VIOLENT DELIGHTS

A DARK BILLIONAIRE ROMANCE

LINNEA MAY

ISBN-13: 978-1547180929
ISBN-10: 1547180927

"These violent delights have violent ends
And in their triumph die, like fire and powder,
Which as they kiss consume: the sweetest honey
Is loathsome in his own deliciousness."
– William Shakespeare

JOSEPH

She is the best one yet.

I have played this game with many girls before, but no one ever caught my attention like she does.

She's waiting for me, kneeling with her thighs spread wide, her perky ass resting on her ankles, her back already arched, chest pushed forward, her neck stretched, her head held high, and the focus of her eyes is lowered to the floor. Her hands are resting, palms up, on her thighs.

The perfect pose of the pleasure slave.

Her chest is heaving in a steady rhythm and her eyelashes flicker when she notices me approaching.

It's the most alluring sight.

My Pet.

There is a dark side to everyone, they say. While that may be true, I doubt that most people's dark sides even come close to those that cast their sinister shadow over the part of myself that I keep hidden.

I'm consumed by the fury of a raging beast, something so dark and violent that even I was scared of myself once. I tried to ignore its existence, tried to push it away, but the effort was futile and only led to more chaos.

However, I am no longer that furious boy I used to be.

Violence has always been a part of my life, but it no longer controls me.

Now I'm the one in control.

I know who I am, I know how to deal with the beast raging inside, and I know what I need. I found what helps me to cope, and no one has to become part of it, unless they want to.

This is what's at the heart of it all.

Choice.

Consent.

Rules.

A safe setting.

Every time I browse through the catalog of women who are willing to offer themselves to me, I am confronted with the reality of human psychology. For every sick person out there with these dark desires and needs, there is someone else who is willing to serve those demands. Together they meet the needs of each other's twisted minds and bodies.

We humans, as a species, are pretty fucked up.

It's a glorious thing.

My Pet is here because she chose to be here, even though the reality of it may frighten her. She agreed to my offer to buy her, and she's proving to be the perfect Pet, tailored exactly to fit my desires.

I have been this agency's client long enough for them to understand my personal tastes right down to the most minute detail. They know what I want from these women, they know what I will do to them, they know what traits a woman must possess, not only in regards to her physical attributes, but also her psychological makeup. And they know what I am willing to pay to satisfy my wishes.

Thirty-nine days, just the two of us, no safe word, no escape. Absolute surrender to my will.

She has entered a world of contradictions, a mix of freedom and discipline doled out in equal measure. One cannot exist without the other. She remains under the agency's protection, as do I.

However, these thirty-nine days belong to me, and there is little to no way for her to break the established routine. I want to make every second count.

I don't like interruptions. I need for both of us to be totally immersed, otherwise our arrangement doesn't serve its purpose.

Its purpose to fulfill my darkest needs.

To satisfy my desires.

To keep me sane.

We are playing a game that few are able to handle. It's more than just simple role playing in the bedroom. This feels as real as it can get. The only difference is that she knows she will get out alive at the end of it. She will return to freedom, to real life, and be an incredibly wealthy woman once our thirty-nine days are over, and she will never hear from me again.

This is how it works, and this is how it *has* to work.

She lets out a soft sigh when I caress her cheek, leaning gently into my touch instead of jerking away from it as she did only a few days ago.

She is different. Her defiance seems real, her struggle at times too much to bear, even for me.

She is here to be trained, for me to hurt her, to teach her. But I struggle to maintain my harsh demeanor. I struggle to train and inflict torture on her as I did to all the others before.

Because there is something special about her. Something that makes all of this feel so very fucking wrong.

Something is off with her. Very, very off.

CHAPTER 1

LIANA

This has been the worst week of my life. You may think I am exaggerating, but I am not.

Everything went to shit this week. That is the plain and simple truth.

It's 10 p.m. on a Friday night, and I'm sitting at the bar of a rundown neighborhood joint, sipping on a cheap bourbon and feeling sorry for myself. I hate bourbon, I've never been to this place before and I'm comically overdressed. I bet half of the slobs here think I am a hooker, because I look so out of place.

I don't even know where I am. I have never been in this area of the city before. I just ended up in this place after wandering the streets for hours, lost in thought and unwilling to go back to my empty house. Walking keeps me in balance, it always has. It's as if the dark thoughts can't catch me as long as I just keep moving, walking. I don't want to go home and face the horrors of this past week.

Faced with the prospect of spending the weekend in my empty place, I had started walking as soon as I left the office, but quickly realized that my heels are not meant for this. I couldn't take them off because it's too cold, so I just stumbled into the first bar I came to, which was this little shit hole. I've been dwelling in my pain for the past hour, staring at nothing and drinking this God-awful bourbon, afraid to go home.

It's pathetic, I know, but so appropriate, considering the turn my life has taken.

I'm not saying my life was glorious before. No, it definitely wasn't. But I had been content and felt no need to change anything. First of all, I had a job. Nothing special. I wasn't changing the world or anything, but it paid the bills and I enjoyed it. I worked at the university as the secretary to a muddle-headed professor. He may have been brilliant in his field, but he was unable to master simpler things, such as responding to emails, creating PowerPoint presentations, and searching the university's intranet.

Professor Miller appreciated my work. He was the nicest man I've ever met, always greeting me with a smile, and he was so easy to impress with simple things that come easy to any millennial. He was an older gentleman with very polite manners, who thanked me profusely for every little thing I did. Working for him was easy, it was predictable. My job with him was the safe constant I needed in my life.

And now it's gone.

He's gone.

Professor Miller died in an accident, hit by a passing car as he was crossing the street, lost in his own world and not paying attention. When he died, my job died, as well. Losing him was more than just a pay-the-bills job-related tragedy: I lost my safe and secure haven, the calm and reliable constant in my life that kept me sane after kicking Luke out of my life.

Luke. My ex-boyfriend. The son of a bitch who had the audacity to fuck another girl in *our* bed, and on *our* sheets, when he thought I was out of town. Yes, he really was that stupid. Or maybe I'm the stupid one for trusting him, considering he was always so insecure. Maybe that should have clued me in that maybe *he* was the problem?

I will never forget the expression on his face when I walked through the door. I had arrived back home a day early, because I couldn't stand another minute with my relatives who I had been visiting. I wanted to surprise him, bearing those dumb chocolates he likes, ready to make up from another awful fight we had had the day before I left.

I *did* surprise him, but not in the way I imagined.

I caught him in the act, yet he was the one who'd accused me time and again of cheating, because of my "sick" needs, as he put it. He never understood me. He lacked the decency to even *listen* to me when I tried to talk with him about it. Every time I summoned the courage to talk about my deepest desires, he looked at me with that appalled and disgusted look on his face and told me that I needed therapy. As if I wasn't feeling weird enough about it already.

I should have known that we weren't meant to be together, but still I clung on, hoping that eventually things would work out. I couldn't let go of him, or rather, I couldn't let go of the idea of us together. In a way, I should be grateful that this happened. Finding him screwing another girl was just the kick I needed to finally free myself of him.

My week started by throwing Luke out of the apartment that we've been living in together for more than nine months—and my week ended with me losing my job when my boss was killed. Everything happened so fast, one atrocious thing after another. I caught Luke on Sunday, threw him out on Monday, Professor Miller was hit by a car on Wednesday and died on Thursday, and today I was told that I will no longer be needed once the professor's office is cleaned out.

Everybody was visibly upset about Professor Miller's death—his colleagues, the assistants, the students—but they all treated me like I was a machine, as if I wouldn't mourn his death just as much as they did. After all, I'm just a secretary, not his academic equal, and I wouldn't be someone who had any close ties to him—or so they think. While others cried, walked around in shock, and consoled one another, I was bombarded with things that had to be organized and done. The cherry on top was when I was called into the Dean's office and advised that because the funding for my position was tied directly to his teaching position—and since the position wouldn't be filled until a national search was conducted and it could take up to a year—my secretarial position was no longer needed. Seriously?

So here I am. Drinking shitty bourbon in a shitty bar. All by myself. Drowning in self-pity at the mess that is my life.

It doesn't help that this woman is sitting across from me. That damn Barbie doll with her ridiculous bright red fur coat. It's so hideous-looking, but it's a perfect match for its owner. She looks just like the girl I caught Luke with. A dumb blonde, with fake lashes, fake nails, fake tits, fake everything. Her fat lips are painted in a ridiculously bright hooker red that matches her ugly fur coat. I bet she really is a hooker. She's by herself, sipping on a bourbon just like I am, and constantly checking the time and watching the door of the bar. She's probably waiting for a john.

I was already here when she walked in, and she caught my attention from the start, not only because of that hideous coat and her resemblance to that other bitch, but because she was wearing a black mask when she came in. It was covering up most of her face. As soon as she sat down, she took it off and placed it on the counter right next to her drink.

She makes me furious. Women like her make me furious. I watch her as she sips on her drink, leaving red lipstick marks on the glass, and constantly shifting her attention between checking her phone and staring at her manicured nails coated in blood red. She has what many men would consider to be the perfect body and a beautiful face—as far as I can tell with all that glob she has plastered on it—but her entire get-up and attitude screams total lack of respect—for herself and anyone else.

She's the kind of woman who destroys—destroys families, destroys reputations, destroys hopes and dreams—and betrays everything that's honorable.

I don't know if it's the effects of the cheap bourbon, the general misery streaming through my veins from my fucked-up life, or the hatred this woman provokes in me by triggering the memory about Luke, but when Barbie doll gets down from her high chair to head for the restroom, I find myself getting up from my seat, as well.

I want to hurt her. I want to share my fucking misery with her, even if it's only through a small and simple act. My body is moving all on its own, driven by blind and rabid fury, as I walk over to take that hideous red fur coat from the back of her empty chair and walk away with it, out the door, and into the dark night.

CHAPTER 2

LIANA

W hy did I just do that? As soon as I walk out the door of the bar, I begin to question my actions. But I don't turn around.

Instead, I wrap the giant red fur coat around my shoulders and start scurrying briskly down the street. I'm pressing my little purse against my side, clutching it with one hand, holding the coat with the other. I'm not in prime shape, so I find myself starting to pant after just a few yards. Only after turning a corner do I feel safe enough to slow my gait to walking.

I am gasping for air—though trying not to attract too much attention—and breaking a sweat, but my feet continue to carry me down the sidewalk. This is not the safest area of the city to be in, and I probably shouldn't be walking all by myself out here, especially at dusk, but I'm not worried enough to hail a cab.

What is safety, anyway?

I thought my job was safe. I thought I was—kind of—safe in my relationship with Luke.

Who says I'd be any less *safe* here? Alone, at night, on a street in a rough neighborhood.

After all, I'm the one who just committed a crime, and a dumb one at that. Even through my sweating and panting, I still find myself holding the red fur coat wrapped around my small body closed with clenched fingers. I'm a rather short person, and this coat is way too big for me, but it protects me from the cold a lot better than my own coat did—the coat I left on the back of my stool at the bar because I was so focused on stealing this one. I'm sure they have a lost and found, and I can just come back tomorrow to fetch it. No harm, no foul.

Or Barbie doll will take it once she realizes hers has disappeared, which then would make this a simple exchange and not a theft. And she's definitely the one who made out better on the deal, if you ask me.

What is this atrocity I am wearing, anyway? It feels warm, but itchy and artificial. At least it's not real fur.

When I bury my hands into the coat's pockets to keep them warm, I feel the thickness of a folded-up piece of paper. I produce what turns out to be a small business card. Just as I suspected, this coat's owner appears to be a sex worker, but more of a high-class kind of escort than what I suspected. Apparently, she goes by the unimaginative name Ruby Red, which may explain the hideous coat. I didn't know escorts had business cards. Who do they give those to? Are there like parties or something, where they meet up with "like-minded" people and exchange contacts for future use?

I furrow my eyebrows and roll my eyes at that idea and turn the card over to see if there's anything written on the back. There are only two words, written in curly calligraphy: *Violent Delights.*

Is that her motto? A promise? I wonder what it means.

I put the card back in the pocket, and as I continue walking, I am reminded why I ended up in that bar in the first place. Not only is it extremely cold out, but my feet also hurt from all the walking I did earlier. I am not used to wearing heels all day. The only reason I wore them today was because they are the only shoes I have that match my black suit. Out of respect, I wanted to wear something black and formal today because I know Professor Miller would have appreciated it. He was always one for tradition and etiquette. This is my way of showing my respect to him.

I can practically see his kind and paternal smile.

A single tear rolls down my cold cheek as my thoughts wander to him. I will miss this man, my boss, my mentor, in some regard. He taught me many things, but most of all, he gave me a place that made me feel stable and secure.

"Thank you."

The words escape my lips in a faint whisper. He thanked me so much, for so many things, even small things, like printing out a simple e-mail. He always wanted his e-mails printed out each morning and placed in a neat pile in the middle of his desk, that's how old-school he was. If it wasn't on paper, it wasn't real.

I turn up the huge collar of the hideous coat and start walking faster. I'm getting more and more miserable out here in the cold and need to find the next subway station, or call a cab.

I take in my surroundings. The area I am walking in is empty and scary at night. There are no other pedestrians, and even vehicles appear to be a rarity. It's time for me to find out exactly where I am so I can get home.

I stop for a moment, turning and searching for anything that would help me figure it out, a street sign, a bus station. But I can't seem to find anything.

Just as I continue hurrying down the sidewalk, I hear a car approaching me from behind. I only notice it because it's driving at a very slow speed. Other cars have passed by me, but they were traveling at what I would consider to be a normal speed. This one is making me a bit nervous because the driver seems to be slowing down, almost as if he's following me.

I don't dare turn around to look to see if he wants anything from me. That's rule number one on the street: no eye contact. Instead, I walk even faster and try to exude confidence, indicating that I won't have his shit and have no interest in talking to him.

The car keeps following me.

There's no corner to turn down, no narrow alley through which I could disappear, no storefront to enter.

My heart begins to race. What is going on? Should I turn around? Should I yell at him to leave me alone?

But I don't get to do any of those things. Before I can do anything, I am grabbed from behind by two incredibly strong arms.

I gasp in shock, unable to even scream because I am so overwhelmed by the abruptness of everything.

A man of ample size and strength wraps his arms around me, pulling me off my feet as he proceeds to drag me with him. I lose my balance, my arms helplessly flying up in the air, as I try to regain control.

And just as I find the will to shriek out in horror, the assailant presses a wet handkerchief over my mouth and nose, forcing me to inhale a pungent substance that turns the world black.

CHAPTER 3

JOSEPH

I wonder if this is what normal people feel like before they embark on a first date. The excitement, nervous anticipation of what's to come. I can't imagine that their feelings even come close to what I'm feeling when I head out to collect my toy.

There is never a set day or time, but always a window of when it will happen, a window of five days. I don't want her to know *exactly* when it will happen, because it would ruin the surprise and affect her behavior. I want a raw and natural reaction when I take her, actual shock, actual fear.

However, the woman has to be prepared for me to take her—she has to be in a proper state, clean and waxed, equipped with certain things I want to see when she comes with me.

And one special item of her choosing. I know she will get lonely at some point, they always do. No matter how well prepared they feel, or how much they actually enjoy being in my possession, they all reach a point when it becomes too much to handle, when they wish for normalcy and a reminder of who they are outside of their temporary cage.

Whatever it is they need in that moment to calm and reassure themselves, I want them to have it. But just that one item. In some cases, I never found out what the woman had chosen to bring with her. Other times, it turned out to be obvious, such as a stuffed animal, a certain item of clothing, or some kind of memento. I may do unspeakable things to them, but I will *never* strip them of this one item. It's one of the clear lines that I draw for myself, the line I draw to keep them sane and connected to the outer world.

Most of them expect me to come for them in the dark, which is why they scurry through the streets like little rabbits that are being chased, always throwing hurried looks over their shoulder to see if someone is following them. It's fun to watch, but I never catch them this way. They feel safer during the day, while they're out running mundane errands such as grocery shopping, or chatting with neighbors as they walk their dogs. They never check behind their backs then, and while it is harder to kidnap a woman during broad daylight, there is *always* a window of opportunity, a brief moment when they are oblivious and not expecting it, but they're also out of sight of others.

The perfect moment to seize them.

That moment hasn't happened with this one yet. My current prey is a perfect Barbie doll with blonde hair and svelte curves, who goes by the name Ruby Red. She is not only easily recognizable because of her striking red fur coat, but also very alert. The coat is her one distinctive feature, the token that sets her apart from everyone else.

Just like all the women before her, she was instructed to move around outside as much as possible—at least six hours per day, any time of the day, day or night—but she wasn't supposed to draw attention by doing anything too out of the ordinary. She doesn't have a day job that I'm keeping her away from—she is a full time escort, just like the others.

Ruby appears to be a true night owl, and it's obvious she has no intention of changing her habits. I have been observing her for three days, and she's rarely outside before dusk. Tonight is no different. Much to my dismay, she has frequented a shit hole bar every single night since I started watching her. I don't like drinkers, something I clearly stated in my requirements. Nothing about her profile indicated she drank, so I am assuming it's new, perhaps something she developed this week to cope with the stress that comes with an arrangement like this. She seemed a lot more harried than any of the others, more frazzled, more worried. Definitely flighty—none of the others have spent as much time looking around as she does, moving like a nervous squirrel. Just tonight, she scurried down the street before disappearing into that bar, her refuge of choice, it seems.

I considered following her inside, to do things a little different than I have with the others. But that would be breaking protocol. I hate breaking the rules, especially the ones I've set up for myself, and the rules clearly state that it has to framed as an abduction with no prior contact. No chit-chat, no winking, not even any looking at her face. I like the mystery of not knowing.

I want to see her face at the same time she sees her cage for the first time. It's a magical moment, one of the best, and almost better than some of the orgasms I will enjoy with her.

And it can only be that special if I don't know too much beforehand. The girls are always asked to hide their faces behind a fabric mask that covers most of their features. It may be awkward for them to walk around like this, but that's not my concern.

It is equally important that they don't see me coming. Ruby, with her constant turning and watching and searching, was a little annoying in that regard. She is making it surprisingly easy tonight, though I am not prepared when she suddenly darts out of the bar half an hour sooner than she usually does. I only notice her when she has already turned her back to me, walking in hurried steps and, for a change, not looking anywhere but straight ahead, as she practically flees from the bar.

What's going on with her? Did she get in trouble? Did someone harass her?

I start the car and follow her, as I always do. Usually, I have to be extremely careful because of her nervous behavior, but tonight she doesn't waste a second looking behind her. She seems to be acting differently.

And it offers me the perfect opportunity.

CHAPTER 4

JOSEPH

She struggles a lot more than any of the others have. Her desperate attempts to fend me off are like an unsuspecting victim who is trying everything to prevent the inevitable. If I hadn't pressed the soaked cloth against her face fast enough, she would have yelled out for help, even though that's not part of the plan. She can struggle, she can try to fend me off, but she cannot make any noise to attract the attention of bystanders.

Her limbs go soft within seconds, and all her weight drops into my arms as she loses consciousness. I have to act fast because she won't be out for long, and I'm not too familiar with this part of town. There could be people walking by any moment now.

I quickly drag her over to the car, lift her up and lay her down on the backseat. I scan my surroundings to make sure no one witnessed this, before hurrying over to the driver's side, positioning myself behind the wheel.

My pulse is racing when I push down on the gas pedal and drive away from the scene as fast as possible. This rush of adrenalin is all part of it. The worry about getting caught, her short but intense struggle, having her in the back of my car, helpless, and soon to be at my mercy. The entire time I'm driving to my place, I'm worried that someone might follow us, or someone might see her motionless body in the back seat when I have to stop at a red light. Anything. There are so many things that could go wrong.

But none of them happen.

Her daze will only last long enough for me to get her home. I glance back at her through the rear mirror time and again, just to make sure that she really is still passed out. Some of them don't inhale enough and simply faint due to the shock of being abducted. In those cases, they awaken within five minutes, and it's always a risk without any restraints.

But in her case, the drug seems to have worked. She doesn't wake up the entire drive. It takes almost an hour for me to get out of the city and reach my residence on the outskirts.

My domestic staff has been informed that this week marks the beginning of another "thirty-nine," a code word they invented to let each other know. None of them know the full extent of what I do with these women, but they are up to speed with as many details as they need to know. They know about the agency and the kind of services I take advantage of. They have to know the bare minimum so I can have the space I need, that we need.

But they don't have to know everything about it, and most of them don't—or wouldn't—even want to. They merely think of it as me having a secretive play partner for thirty-nine days every so often. "Thirty-nine" is their signal to stay out of my way as much as possible. None of them ever enter the uppermost floor, and only one of my staff has ever even seen the rooms up there. Marcus, the head of my cleaning crew, had to sign a full disclosure agreement before I hired him for this particular job, so if he ever jabbers to anyone about it, he understands the seriousness of the consequences he will be dealt.

The house is completely empty tonight, just as I have asked. My staff won't return until I call for them. My beautiful renovated Victorian mansion awaits at the end of the dark driveway, seemingly harmless, but filled with all the tools I need to fulfill my darkest desires.

I park the car in the driveway and pause for a moment, my eyes glued to the rearview mirror. I can see her laying on the back seat, still unconscious and unaware of what will happen to her over the next thirty-nine days. She may have signed up for this voluntarily, she may even be into this sort of thing —or she is just here to endure a little more than a month of tortuous and sadistic hardship in exchange for an amount of money unattainable through traditional means. After this, she may never have to work again, if she doesn't want to.

Eventually, I will get to know all about her, her secrets, her fears, her desires, her dreams. I will be as close to her as anyone has ever been before, and I will make her do things she never thought possible. I will expose a new side of her, a side that will be exclusively mine. Forever. Even after we're done here, that side will remain with me, and she will share things with me that she would never share with anyone else.

They all do.

It's all part of it. The pain, the sex, the intimacy, the humiliation, the revelation.

My impatient body craves her without even having seen her face. The tension of the first few days is one of the best parts. It may take days until I fuck her, but my cock is already yearning to be buried deeply inside her, straining painfully against its fabric cage, as I get out of the car and walk around to the passenger side.

The first thing I notice when I open the door to the back seat is that she's not wearing her mask. I can only see parts of her face because it's hidden behind the massive collar of her fur coat and her tousled hair.

I only catch a glimpse before I tear my eyes away, cursing as I turn around.

Why the fuck is she not wearing her mask?

I avert my eyes and wonder what I should do. She isn't even inside the house yet, but she has already amassed two strikes for punishment. Drinking and forgetting to wear her mask. This hasn't happened before.

Breathe, I tell myself. I clench my fists in anger and close my eyes, as I take in three deep, cleansing breaths to calm myself.

She will get punished, but in due time. And I won't ruin this for myself by looking at her face before I am ready, before it's time.

I grunt with anger as I take off my scarf and open the door to the car again, making sure not to look directly at her as I wrap the garment around her face.

Done.

I saved myself from immense disappointment, and cannot help but smile as I carry her inside, eagerness building in my gut for the actual reveal.

CHAPTER 5

LIANA

I feel as if I've drowned in a big puddle of mud, immersed in a numbing darkness that pulsates inside me and around me like the heart of a giant beast. When I try to open my eyes, they refuse, as do my limbs when I try to move. They lay limp and heavy on the ground, as I realize that I am sprawled out on a wooden floor, unable to move or even see where I am.

There is no sound and no light, but there *is* pain. I have a blazing headache.

As I try again to open my heavy eyelids, I realize they are covered by something that's been wrapped around my head. A soft and warm piece of fabric that's pressed tightly against my skin, pushing my eyes shut and only leaving a small slit right below my mouth to allow me to breathe.

What the hell is this? What happened? Where am I?

I want to verbalize all these questions, but I can't. When I try to speak, I'm suffocated by the same scarf that's keeping my eyes shut. I need to get it off of me.

A strange-sounding groan leaves my mouth when I send another command for my arms to lift. This time, they obey. My hands feel as heavy as dumbbells when I move them up to my face to remove the blinding scarf. I expect there to be light once I manage to unwrap my head as well as I can without lifting my tired and throbbing head, but there is hardly any. I'm still consumed by darkness.

I find myself staring around a very dimly lit room when the scarf is removed. The only thing I can see clearly is a ceiling far above me, and a pitch of the roof to my side. A single light bulb is dangling from the ceiling and providing what little light there is. It provides nothing more than a low glimmer that helps me recognize contours and vague orientation of the room around me.

Wherever I am, it's in a room on the uppermost floor of a rather old building with high ceilings and a wooden floor.

I remain on the floor, as if my body was nailed down to it. A terrible sense of foreboding sends trickles of fear through my veins, and it forbids me from moving.

Where is this? How did I get here?

I lazily turn my head to the side, only to find an empty wall about three feet away from me. There is nothing there, only a wall.

But then I notice something.

I'm not alone.

I hear another breath joining the faint sound of mine.

I roll my head to the other side and almost let out a shriek of panic when I see him. Suddenly, my entire body is painfully awake and my mind suddenly aware of the danger I might be in.

I jerk up to a sitting position so suddenly that I escape unconsciousness only by a whisker. An aching vertigo claims me as I tumble backward until my back is brushing against the empty wall, and I hold up one hand in a silly attempt of protection.

A short and violent cry fills the room as I try to cope with everything at once, the confusion, the pain in my head, that fucking dizziness, and the realization that there is a strange man sitting at the other end of the room.

Who the hell is he? Did he bring me here?

For what seems like an agonizingly long time, we just stare at each other while tense silence stretches between us. My eyes needed a while to get accustomed to the dim lighting, but now that they are, I cannot only detect the shape of the man sitting across from me, but I also get a better picture of the room we're in. It's small, the roof sloping on three sides, and there is only one very small window, which appears to be closed with a shade on the outside. An attic, that's what this must be. I am in some-one's attic.

Probably *his* attic. The man is sitting on the floor, less than ten feet away from me, his legs crossed and palms resting on his knees, and his dark eyes are fixated on me. Even in his sitting position, I can tell that he must be rather tall, and powerfully strong. His shoulders are broad, and his upper arms stretch the material of the gray shirt he's wearing, his muscles forming prominent lines.

All things considered, I have to admit that he is stun-ningly handsome. His dark eyes, thick eyebrows, and defined cheekbones give him a very sharp and mature look, even though he doesn't seem to be that much older than me. A peppered stubble graces his chiseled jaw, and strong, dark strands of hair partly hide the left side of his face, as he wears it in a casual side-swept. It's hard to tell many details under these circumstances, but I know that he is shockingly gorgeous. He would have taken my breath away anywhere else, but right now he does nothing but scare the hell out of me.

"Who are you?" I croak.

My hoarse voice breaks the silence between us, and even though it was nothing more than a whisper, my question comes out awfully loud and intrusive. I almost wish I hadn't spoken.

He doesn't reply, but I can see the hint of a smirk fleeting across his face.

Does my misery amuse him? Who *is* this sick bastard?

Instead of answering my question, he continues staring at me, the expression on his handsome face changing from a mischievous glare to a smile that frightens me even more.

I flinch when he suddenly rises to his feet, his impressive height towering over me.

"Beautiful," he says with a deep, but low voice.

"Perfect."

CHAPTER 6

JOSEPH

This must be the best one yet. Her horror seems so real, so raw and natural. It's easy to forget that most of this is all an act. Her widened eyes when she gazes through the room speak of nothing but fear and confusion, and they are set in the most beautiful face I have ever had in my house.

She looks younger than I expected, way younger. I usually order them slightly older than me, because that is what I typically go for. Older women with experience, mature enough to make responsible decisions, but still physically firm and young enough to be attractive and keep my attention. Her file said that she was in her early thirties, but her face looks like that of a girl in her early twenties.

It's been less than ten minutes since I placed her unconscious body on the floor, already coming to know the feel of her in my arms as I carried her up the stairs from the car. She is shorter than I expected, and not very heavy. I did nothing but bring her up here and lay her down on the floor. While I'm haunted by a wide range of twisted thoughts and ideas, necrophilia is not among them. I take no joy in abusing her body in this helpless state.

I need her awake to fully enjoy her. And I want to be there with her to watch her when she opens her eyes for the first time.

My heart skipped a beat when a subtle motion and an even fainter moan suggested she was about to regain consciousness. The drug only acts for a very limited time, but it's hard to shake it off completely right away. Even with that knowledge, it was a joy to watch her struggle as she slowly comes to herself and fights to get the scarf off of her face.

I held my breath when she finally revealed that face I have been so eager to see. My eyes are fixated on her every breath as she takes in her surroundings for the first time, her eyes locked on the ceiling above her in a blank stare as her scattered mind tries to make sense of her situation. Even when they know this will happen, they are still shocked to find themselves actually here. Nothing can prepare a person for this, nothing. They only understand after waking up in a dark attic, lying on the floor with nothing but the things they had with them when I took them.

Just as required, she is dressed up beneath the red fur coat, wearing a dark ladies' suit with a tight-fitting skirt that is driving me crazy. The protocol dictates that they wear stockings underneath that skirt, and I can't wait to see them as I push up her skirt for the very first time.

Soon.

It only takes her a few moments to fully regain consciousness, and she's back with a bang when she sees me sitting next to her. I suppress a chuckle as she jumps up like a frightened deer and scuttles away from me until she can go no further.

And then she concludes our first encounter with the perfect question.

"Who are you?"

Next to "Where am I?", this must be the most often posed question for a victim to ask their kidnapper after waking up from a drug-induced slumber. What a good girl she is, playing the part to perfection.

The girls are instructed to act as if this really happened out of nowhere, unexpectedly. Not all of them stick to protocol, though. More than once I've had to put them back into place, inflicting enough terror to make them realize that this is not a joke. It's not a silly game between lovers who got bored of each other in the bedroom. There is no breaking character, no escaping, no joking when you forget the lines. None of that.

This one, Ruby, appears to understand that. I like her already, despite her earlier misconduct. My slave training follows the carrot-and-stick policy: every misstep will be followed up with punishment, while compliance will be met with a treat.

The fear written all over her young face turns to panic when I stand up and rise to stand above her, my eyes never leaving the shivering and scared little person she has turned into.

"Beautiful," I say. "Perfect."

They are never able to appreciate a compliment when they first enter this dark world of captivity under my roof. Ruby, just like so many before her, only furrows her eyebrows, her tiny nose wrinkling as if she's confronted with an unpleasant smell.

"You will call me Master," I announce. "Do you understand?"

Her eyes widen with a new wave of terror.

"What?" she gasps. "Where am I? What is this?"

Her voice is trembling, and her face turning into a grimace as if she's about to cry.

She's brilliant.

"Tell me you understand," I tell her. "You will call me Master. Understand?"

A horrified gasp escapes her lips when I approach closer, taking only one single step.

"Why would I...? Who the hell are you?!" she hisses at me.

Okay, now she's taking it too far. I want to put her in her place, but I can't break character either. I won't remind her of the contract she signed, the contract that clearly states she's giving up any freedom and free will while she's my captive. That contract also stated how she is to address me, and I don't feel like spelling it out to her again.

I dart forward, too quickly for her to react before I get my hands on her. She shrieks in horror when I pin her against the wall she's been leaning up against, grabbing her by the throat without actually choking her, and using my other hand to keep her held in place. She's too shocked to fight back, her terrified eyes fixating on me as she comes to terms with the fact that there is nothing she can do to escape my grip.

"Do you understand?" I repeat my question, emphasizing every word.

She whimpers and her lower lip begins to tremble, her eyes watering with despair.

This I can work with. Raw terror and desperation. She's good.

I tighten my grip around her throat, pushing her further back against the wall, while moving my face so close to hers that I can feel her anxious breath on my skin.

"Yes," she breathes. "Yes, yes, yes."

She hesitates, leaving a moment for the first of many tears to roll down her delicate cheek.

"Yes, Master," she adds.

I smile at her.

"Good girl."

CHAPTER 7

LIANA

W hat the hell is happening to me? I'm so confused, overwhelmed with questions and an anxiety that runs deeper than mere bewilderment about my current situation and how I got here.

This is fucked-up on so many levels that I don't even know where to start. When he comes at me, his strong hand clutching around my throat just enough to send a warning without really hurting me, I'm not only horrified because he's threatening me.

I'm not just afraid of *him*—I'm afraid of myself.

I should be nothing but terrified, I should scream for help and at least try to fend him off, until I can't fight him. I should cry, I should kick him, I should head for the door and try everything within my power to get out of this room, to escape.

That is how I *should* feel.

Scared. Horrified. In panic and tears.

I should *not* be excited about this. I should not be turned on.

Nothing about this is appealing. I was ambushed, drugged and kidnapped to a spooky attic, and am being held down and intimidated by a daunting stranger.

A man who looks like a fucking god.

A man whose hand feels alarmingly good braced around my throat.

No!

I close my eyes, trying to shake off those sick thoughts. *What is wrong with me*?!

"Look at me!" he barks, as soon as my eyes shut.

I oblige immediately, met with his dark gaze right in front of my face. I can't help it. He looks fucking gorgeous.

Did someone set this up for me? Is he being paid to fulfill a fantasy so dark that no one ever dares to explore it?

Is that why I can't be entirely scared of him? Because I don't believe it's real?

But who would do such a thing? No one even knows about those twisted dreams I've had. No one knows that I've been fantasizing about something like this for years. No one but Luke, and I'm positive that he has nothing to do with this.

Unless this is his way of punishing me. Did he hire someone to make this come true, only to scare the hell out of me and show me how sick I am for wanting this?

Is that it?

My stream of thoughts is interrupted by a sharp pain when the man, who I am to call Master, lifts my face up to his while still holding my throat.

He looks at me, wondering, waiting, studying every inch of my face. I have never been looked at like this before. There is an intensity to his gaze that is new to me, and for the first time in my life, I begin to understand what people mean when they say that someone's look is piercing. He observes me with such depth that his gaze feels like a touch, just as much as his hand does.

"Now, you will listen to me," he whispers. "From now on, you're mine. You'll do as I say, no backtalk, no objections, no arguing. It's as simple as that. You'll forget everything you were outside of this house. Your name, your friends, your family, your hobbies. You'll just exist to please me."

He pauses for a moment, waiting for me to react to his insane demands, but I don't give him anything but a blank stare.

"You no longer have a name," he adds. "From now you'll just be *Pet*. My Pet. Understand?"

Again, he pauses, waiting for my reply. I suggest a nod, but can't move my head enough, because he's still pinning me firmly in place.

"Yeah," I croak, annoyed at the weak sound of my voice.

I thought this is what he wanted to hear, but instead of a pleased smile, he squeezes my throat even harder, taking my breath away for real this time. I moan in pain and my arms fly up, instinctively reaching for his arm in an attempt to get him away from me. Of course, this is futile. He doesn't even flinch or acknowledge my defense in any way, but his pressure doesn't loosen.

I can't breathe! He's going to choke me!

I want to warn him that he's actually hurting me, that I will faint any minute now, if he keeps this up. Maybe that's what he wants? Is he trying to kill me?

But just when I feel actual panic emerging, he lets go of me, withdrawing his hand from my throat, and ready to catch me as I collapse forward, coughing and gasping for air.

"What did I tell you to call me?" he asks with a calm and steady voice, entirely unfazed by my desperate struggle for air and the obvious pain he inflicted upon me.

Shit. This man is seriously disturbed.

I try to speak, but I can't. My throat is sore from his violent treatment and I am caught in another coughing fit as I try to give him the reply I hope he'd rather hear.

"Master," I finally manage to utter. "Master. You said I should call you Master."

He's holding me by the shoulders and sets me upright with a gentle push. My chest is still heaving in abrupt bursts, when I look up at him, met with a stoic expression that makes my blood run cold.

"That's right," he says. "When I ask you to do something, you don't say 'Yeah', you say, 'Yes, Master.' Understand?"

I cast him a sinister look. This is ridiculous. He must know that. Why would I just agree to any of this before he gives me an explanation?

"Where am I?" I ask. "Who are you? Did Luke send you?"

He furrows his eyebrows and lets out an angry growl that is probably supposed to scare me. But I only react when he squeezes my shoulders, a subtle yet effective warning on how much power he possesses over me.

"I am losing my patience with you," he hisses through gritted teeth. "And trust me, you don't want that to happen. So, let's try this again. You will listen to me, obey me, please me, and you will address me as your Master. Do you understand?"

The grip on my shoulders intensifies. I squint, fighting an internal struggle between defiance and fright. I have no need for further pain, but I also refuse to just go along with his ridiculous demands before I get an explanation as to what this is all about.

But maybe the only way for me to get an explanation is to go along with his wishes. For now.

"Yes, Master," I whisper, lowering my eyes in defeat. "Yes, Master. I understand."

CHAPTER 8

JOSEPH

I'm inclined to call her a good girl again, but decide that she doesn't quite deserve that yet. She's been more of a struggle than most, if not all, of her predecessors.

And who the hell is Luke? If this was some guy from the agency, shouldn't I know him? I assume it must be someone who is only known to the girls, but is never in contact with the clients.

Why would she mention him? She knows that she's not allowed to mention anyone or anything that relates to our deal. She is to act as if this was a real kidnapping. It's supposed to feel as real as it can get.

None of this will work if she keeps overstepping the ground rules. As beautiful and convincing as she is otherwise, I won't forgive her ruining this for me. I will send her back without payment if she doesn't stop asking dumb questions that have no place in this arrangement.

"Now, let's try this again," I say, still holding her by the shoulders. "Your only job is to please me. You exist for me. You'll smile for me, you'll cry for me, you'll beg for me, you'll breathe for me, and most importantly of all, you'll come for me."

Even in the faint light, I can see her cheeks blushing at that last sentence. Good. Despite her temporary forgetfulness, she still seems responsive to me.

"Come for you?" she asks, her chest heaving nervously. "What do you-?"

"I'll show you," I say, reaching forward so I can lift her up and get her away from that restraining wall.

She gasps in surprise when I drag her over to the middle of the empty room, removing the heavy fur coat from her small frame. My Pet is wearing a dark ladies' suit underneath, with matching heels and a white blouse under the tapered suit jacket. I love the view of her elegantly dressed body as it's spread out for me on the wooden floor after I release her. She clumsily supports herself on her elbow as she tries to fix her skirt with the other hand.

Cute.

I slap her hand away, and she regards me with an indignant look.

"That's mine," I tell her, as if further explanation is needed. "Don't you dare hide that body from my eyes.

It's mine now, and I can look at it and touch it however and whenever I want."

She takes in a deep breath of air and furrows her eyebrows. Backtalk is at the tip of her tongue, but she's smart enough not to say anything. Instead, her eyes widen in horror when I lean forward, casting a shadow over her as my hands glide along her upper thighs, pushing the skirt up further, expecting to find the hem of her stockings.

But there are none. She's not wearing what I asked her to wear. Instead of sexy stockings with a decorative garter belt, she's hiding pantyhose beneath her pencil skirt.

I growl with anger. Did she not read her instructions at all? This has never happened before.

Or is she just especially naughty and seeking punishment? Does she get off on misbehaving?

"I ordered a *pet*," I hiss at her. "Not a *brat*."

She casts me a questioning look, as if she has no idea what I am talking about. Her entire body trembles as I move my hands further up her sides, pushing her skirt out of the way and exposing her covered-up center. Not only is she wearing pantyhose, she also didn't obey my order to go without panties.

"You think this will keep you safe from me?" I ask, as my hands move between her legs, stroking along the inside of her upper thighs, so close that I can feel the warmth of her pussy.

A surprised shriek escapes her when I grab her pantyhose by the seam and rip them in one swift motion, exposing the pale flesh of her thighs and black lacey panties underneath. She whimpers and instinctively tries to cover herself, which makes me furious. Once again, I have to push her hands aside, causing her to yelp in protest, while she pushes her legs together to keep me out.

She's not only clumsy, but weak in her movements, so it's easy for me to annul her pathetic attempts by pushing her legs apart with my knees. I grab her wrists and push her back on the floor, keeping her in place with the weight of my body on top of her.

As annoying as her disobedience has been, I fucking love this struggle and her reluctance to give me what I want. I yearn for this chase. My cock is rock-hard with desire, and I can see her blushing as she feels my hardness pressing against her body. Perfect, just perfect.

"You are playing with fire," I warn her, reveling in her tortured grimace as I push her arms down on the wooden floor. "Disobeying orders. Withdrawing what's mine. Is this how you want to do this?"

She looks up at me, breathing rapidly, her eyes wide with sheer terror.

"I don't know what this is," she whimpers. "Where am I? Why am I here?"

Her confusion seems so real that I can't help but be impressed by her acting skills.

"You know what this is," I hiss. "You're mine now. My little fuck toy. And you better start behaving like one from now on. With all the defiance you've shown so far, I don't even know where to begin with your punishment."

"Punishment?" she gasps. "What for? I've not do—"

"Enough!" I interrupt her. "You stop talking now and fucking *obey*! Do you understand?"

She flinches at the volume of my voice. I'm not a yeller. I've never raised my voice to any of these women.

Because I never had to.

At this point, most of them would already be spread naked in front of me, obediently following my demands for the poses I want from them, hoping to please me enough to let them out of this room. That's the first step. I don't just let them walk out of here so they can move into the more comfortable version of the cage. They have to earn it.

And this one is a long way from getting there.

CHAPTER 9

LIANA

"Yes, I understand," I whisper, defeated. "Master."

"Good."

He loosens his grip on my wrists, and I sigh with relief as he straightens himself up, removing his weight from me and coming to kneel between my legs. I remain sprawled out before him, my legs spread, my ripped pantyhose exposing my core to him. I'm trembling and don't dare to move. His touch is fierce and intimidating. He may hurt me if I don't go along with whatever he asks of me. And it has become obvious that he's not in the mood to explain anything.

He's angry. His face, the way he's breathing, and the way he charged at me, all of that is proof enough that he's furious, despite being so calm and collected when I woke up.

I don't understand it. I don't understand why he's so angry at me, why he keeps saying I would be disobeying his orders. What orders? He only told me to call him Master, and I've done that, even though it took a warning to remind me. Why did he get so mad when he pulled my skirt up? How did I disappoint him? Is it me? My body? Was he hoping for something different when he grabbed me off the street?

His eyes are on me, observing, as I tremble before him.

"Undress," he says. "Now."

I frown at him. "Excuse me?"

"Now!" he repeats, his voice so loud that I flinch with fear.

I am so fucking scared that I can't fight my flight instinct and move away from him. I struggle up, supporting myself on my hands as I hurry to crawl away from him, moving like a drunken crab and losing one of my heels in the process. I move until I can go no further and feel another wall pressed against my back.

He doesn't move, but his dark gaze follows me.

"No," I protest, my voice not carrying the conviction I'd rather have him hear. "Let me out. Please, let me go."

He furrows his eyebrows, seemingly confused by my objection. He looks like he just asked for the most normal thing, and I'm refusing to give it to him.

"I will count down from three," he announces. "If you're not getting rid of your clothes by the time I'm done, then that was it."

What was what? What happens when he's done counting down?

"Three," he says, before I find myself able to react.

"What happens if I don't?" I ask. "Will you let me go if I don't?"

"Two," he says, ignoring my question.

I inhale audibly, trying to figure out what I should do. I can't just go along with this without knowing why I am here, how all of this happened, who he is and how he found me. If he wanted to kill me, he'd probably have done it by now, wouldn't he?

Or is that what he's implying? Will he kill me if I don't undress for him?

"Will you kill me?" I ask in a frantic tone. "Is that what's going to happen once you're done counting?"

He looks at me, showing no sign of acknowledging my question or any eagerness to give me a reply.

"One," he says.

I gasp in surprise when he suddenly rises up to his feet, his eyes leaving me for the first time since I've regained consciousness. He turns his back to me and heads for the door. I curse myself when he turns the doorknob and it becomes apparent that the door has not been locked. I could have run outside the entire time! I'm so freaking dumb!

He opens the door and walks out, quickly closing it behind himself, and even though a loud and clear click sound announces that he's locking it this time, I jump up and run for the door, trying to turn the doorknob right after he has left.

Of course, it doesn't move. I'm locked in.

"Hey!" I yell, hammering against the door with one hand while I continue to work the doorknob with the other. "Let me out!"

I pause for a moment, stepping back from the door to listen, and to see whether he was just trying to scare me and is coming back.

But he isn't.

I can't hear anything but my own erratic breathing, as I stand a step away from the door, wearing only one shoe, the other still lying on the floor where I lost it, right next to the ridiculous fur coat I stole. I take off my other shoe, as well. My feet are still hurting, and this is not a situation that calls for heels.

I turn around, inspecting the small room calmly now that he's gone. However, there's not much to inspect. The room has two windows under the roof slope, and both of them are sealed with shutters from the outside. I have no idea where I am. I could still be in the middle of the city or somewhere far, far away. I no longer have my purse, and I have no idea if I lost it when he grabbed me, or if he took it from me before bringing me up here.

Like most people, I use my phone to check the time and no longer wear a watch. There's no way for me to know how long I've been knocked out. Just a few minutes? Hours? Days?

It probably hasn't been days. I'm sure my body would feel differently if it had been that long. But I can't even tell if it's still night out, or already morning.

I turn around in a circle, searching for clues, or for anything that could help me get out of here. But there's nothing. There's absolutely *nothing* in this room, except for me and the clothes I was wearing when he took me. I'm cold, so I decide to put on the red fur coat. As hideous as it may be, at least it's warm.

What now? There is absolutely nothing I can do, except for yelling and hammering against the door, until he gets bothered enough to let me out.

So that's what I do.

CHAPTER 10

JOSEPH

I'm confused. Why is she making things so hard for herself? No girl has *ever* refused to get naked in front of me, in hopes that they will please me enough to receive a reward. They know that this is how it works. They obey, they get a treat. And putting them in a place where they have nothing is usually a guarantee for their obedience.

Not with this one. Stubborn little Ruby plays the role of the frightened and confused kidnapping victim so well that she seems to not only forget a lot of her orders, but also exaggerates her defiance.

Getting naked for a man should come easy to her. It's her job. She does it all the time. Why does she refuse to do it for me? What's the point of that?

She is different, that's for sure. Ruby will be the first girl to spend the night in the attic. All others have been allowed to leave the room within minutes. It's always been easy to make them obey and come to terms with their situation while they were still in that room and so eager to get out of there. It's dark, it's cold, and it's uncomfortable. As soon as they were out of there and placed in their bedroom, that's when the real challenge begins. When they are surrounded by cozy sheets and all the luxury they can imagine, that's when they turn into brats, and I have to remind them that none of that is to be taken for granted.

Ruby, however, turned things into a challenge from the start. She's not dressed the way I told her to be dressed, she had a drink, she fails to address me correctly, and she doesn't follow verbal commands. Training her will be more difficult than I expected.

I am standing outside her door, watching it quake as she hammers against it from the other side, yelling for me to let her out. Pathetic.

Even she must know that this will get her nowhere. I'm standing in the hallway, my arms crossed in front of my chest as I watch the door from a few feet away. Her hammering stops for a while, and I listen for her to say anything, but I am greeted with nothing but silence. When I step closer to the door, I can hear her moving around inside the attic. She must have kicked off her second shoe, as well, because I cannot hear heels clicking along the floor, just the faint sound of her bare feet padding across the wood.

She'll get bored soon. There's nothing to see, nothing to do. Even if she erupts into a violent rampage, she wouldn't be able to get out of that room. No one will hear her scream because there's no one around for miles. Except for me. She's too weak to break through the door with its safety lock, and there's no way that she could break either one of the windows. Even if she did shatter the glass, the shutters would prevent her from getting any further.

It only takes her a few moments to figure all of this out on her own, and as soon as she realizes how hopeless her situation is, she's back at the door, banging at it with her small fists and screaming for me to let her out.

I step away from the door, listening to the spectacle for a while, before I decide that I am getting bored of it. It's late and I am getting tired. I'm sure she will wear herself out soon, as well. There are still traces of the narcotic in her system, even though it's minimal at this point. Her anxiety, the confusion, all that adrenaline rushing through her body now that the most terrifying job she ever signed up for has effectively started—all of it combined with her erratic behavior will take its toll soon enough.

She's flinging unintelligible curses at me, worsening her punishment even more. I have no intention of listening to this any longer, so turn around to head downstairs.

"There's no bathroom in here!" I hear her shriek, just as I am about to reach the steps.

I pause, a mischievous smirk gracing my face when I turn around and walk back to her.

"You should have thought of that before!" I yell back at her.

And with that, she turns quiet.

CHAPTER 11

LIANA

I awake curled up in a corner, the giant coat wrapped around me, stiff and cold after what has been the longest night of my life. My entire body hurts from falling asleep in an awkward position, and my right arm fell asleep under the weight of my body. Now it's aching with trickling pins-and-needles pain as my limbs start coming back to life.

I squint around the dimly lit room, still trying to figure out where the hell I am. My disorientation is soon replaced by the horror of realization. A pained groan flees my mouth when I edge up into a sitting position, stretching my sore legs and arms, trying to get the blood flowing again. Why did this have to happen to me while I was wearing the most uncomfortable outfit in my closet? This ordeal would be more bearable if I was wearing sweatpants instead of my tight-fitting suit. The ripped pantyhose leave me exposed to the cold of the room, and I'll be surprised if I don't end up with a bladder infection.

It was the coldest night I've ever had to suffer through. God knows what I would have done without this coat. It was the only comfort under otherwise terrible circumstances. I pull up the collar and close the coat around my tired body. There is no way of knowing what time it is. Did I sleep through the night? How many hours have passed since I finally fell asleep? How many hours passed since that man left the room?

The man I am supposed to call Master.

A pain in my core reminds me of why I woke up. I have to pee, badly. With no access to any kind of bathroom, this is an actual problem.

You should have thought of that before, he said. That asshole.

Before what? Before I decided to be kidnapped and locked up? Before I insisted on asking him questions instead of following his orders like a dumb sheep? He acts as if I'm here of my own free will. How psychotic is this man?

Yet, he is my only way out. For all I know, he may just leave me in here, let me pee myself or starve to death, but I should at least try to get his attention.

"Hey!" I try to yell, but my voice produces nothing but a pathetic croak. My throat is sore from the cold and not having anything to drink... and from when he tightened his hand around it last night before he left.

I clear my throat, trying to strengthen my voice.

"Hey!" I yell again, and this time it's stronger and louder. "I need to pee!"

I wait for any kind of response, but there is none. Nothing but silence.

"Please!" I add. "Please! I won't try anything! I just need to pee!"

Again, nothing. He may not even hear me. There is no way for me to know whether he left me here all by myself, sitting in the locked attic of an empty house that's God knows where.

"Hello?" I ask into the nothingness. "Are you still there? Please let me at least know if you're still there!"

Silence.

"Oh, for fuck's sake," I hiss and get up on my feet. They are cold and stiff, just like the rest of my body, but I didn't put my shoes back on. They may have provided a minimum of warmth, but more than anything, they hurt like hell. I placed them next to the door, neatly positioned next to one another, as if I was just a visitor, ready and able to leave at any time.

"Hey!" I repeat, now banging against the door. "Say something! I know you're there!"

Of course, I don't know if he's here or not, but I feel like it cannot hurt to act confident, even if I am anything but that.

"Say something!" I shriek, accelerating my pounding against the wooden door. That goddamn door.

I stop when my fist begins to hurt and I no longer see a point in hurting myself for nothing. Breathing erratically, I pause and listen, trying to figure out if I really am here alone, or if he is lingering on the other side. I press my ear against the crack between the door and its frame, holding my own breath so it doesn't drown out any noise that might be coming from the other side. For a few moments, I don't hear a single sound, and just when I decide to withdraw in defeat, I can hear a step. Then another.

Frightened, I jump back from the door, bracing myself for him to come inside. But he doesn't show up. Then the sound of approaching steps stops.

"Hello?" I ask, my voice lower than it was before. "You're there. I can hear you."

Again, I am met with nothing but silence. He's there, or rather, *someone* is there. I have no reason to believe that it's anybody but him, and I don't know what would scare me more—seeing him, or some other psychotic creep who might be even worse?

My bladder is killing me, and the stinging pain reminds me that I don't have much time left before I make this situation even worse for myself.

"Please," I say, switching to a pleading tone as I step back to the door. "Please, I'm in pain. Please, please, just let me out to use the restroom."

Nothing.

Desperation spreads through my chest, choking me just as his hand around my throat did last night. I'm close to tears, helpless, weakened, and at a loss with my predicament.

He's right there. He can hear me, but he doesn't react to my pleas. What am I supposed to do? Tears blur my vision as I lower my eyes.

"Please," I beg, my voice so low that I don't even think he can hear me. "Please let me out. I can't go on any longer. Please, please, please..."

My words evolve into sobbing, as I bury my face in my hands, crushed with the loss of my last remaining hope. I'm going to pee myself, and won't that just be the frosting on the cake of what is definitely the most horrible experience of my life? Is that what he wants? For me to utterly humiliate myself? What does he want from me?

Then I realize, there *is* something he said he wanted from me. I look up, my eyes widening with understanding, as tears continue rolling down my face.

"Master," I breathe. "Please, Master. I beg you to let me out."

I pause, holding my breath as I wait for his response.

"I promise to be a good girl," I add.

Not even two seconds pass before I can hear steps approaching on the other side of the door.

CHAPTER 12

JOSEPH

"Will you be a good girl from now on?" I ask, as I step inside and find her standing before me, squinting as the light from the hallway streams into her room.

It's the first time that I get a proper look at her. She was wrapped up in my scarf and bundled up in her coat when I brought her up here, and the poor lighting in this room did not allow me to really see her.

She looks very different from what I expected based on her file. Sure, the last hours have left their mark on her. She looks disheveled and tired, her hair falls down around her shoulders in messy waves, and her makeup is smeared from all the crying. One of the first things I notice is the color of her hair. She's a blonde, just as I prefer, but her hair is darker than it was on the few pictures I saw. I have only seen her in the dark because she hardly ever left the house during the daytime, but I never noticed that her hair color was so different. It's more of a dark ash blonde than a true blonde.

"Please," she pleads, her lower lip quivering. "Master. Please, let me use the restroom."

I watch as she goes down on her knees in front of me, clasping her hands together in front of her chest, sobbing while she looks up at me. "Please."

"Get up," I hiss at her. "That's a pathetic display. You don't ask for things like this."

A trace of bewilderment flashes across her pretty face, but for once, she follows my command without hesitation. She gets back up on her feet and wraps her arms around her torso, all while pressing her legs together.

"You may go," I tell her, and her eyes widen with relief. "If you promise to behave from now on. No backtalk, no questions, no hesitation."

She nods even as I speak.

"Yes, yes, yes," she says hurriedly. "Yes, Master. Anything you want, please just—"

"And you'll wear this," I interrupt her, producing a leather collar from my pocket. It's a very simple design, just a slim, black leather collar with the obligatory d-ring in the front.

I hold it up to her, and I can see her eyes flicker when she realizes what it is. I don't know if it's panic or excitement, and I hope for her sake that it's a little bit of both.

She nods again, remaining still when I close the collar around her neck. It's just a training collar, nothing fancy.

She could even open the clasp herself and take it off on her own volition.

However, it's better for her if she doesn't.

"You cannot take this off," I tell her, after fastening the clasp at the back of her neck. "Never. Understand?"

She looks up at me. "Yes... Master."

"Good girl," I say. "Now come."

I hook my finger around the d-ring and turn around, pulling her with me as I march out of the room. She's a lot shorter than I am, and has trouble keeping up with my long strides. I don't want her to look around too much once we leave her cell. We're heading through a narrow corridor with big windows to the left. I can see her head turning toward them as we move along, squinting at the rising sun. It's early morning, and she has been alone in her cell for about six hours. I didn't get much sleep myself. I never sleep well the first night a new girl is here. There's too much anticipation, too many thoughts running through my head, so much to look forward to— and so much to fear.

I wonder if she slept at all. She stumbles next to me, her hands rising up and holding on to mine as I pull her along by her collar. She tries to ease the tension on her throat by putting her own hands between mine and the collar, but it doesn't do much.

At least this struggle keeps her occupied enough not to pay too much attention to her surroundings. We are leaving the corridor behind us, reaching the open space that has the stairs leading downstairs on the left and another, longer corridor to the right. We take the route to the right, as I lead her to her new home. The entire uppermost floor will be hers, but she won't get to see anything else for the next thirty-nine days. Three doors branch off from this hallway, and that is it.

And the attic she just came from. She may hope never to see that room again, but I doubt this was her last night within its confines.

I stop in front of the last door, quickly unlocking it before I push her inside ahead of me. She has trouble maintaining her balance when I shove her into the bathroom. The room is not very big, but still causes her to gasp in awe when she steps into its interior. I prefer a sleek and modern design for my own living area, but for this bathroom, which will only be used by the girls, I've hired an interior designer to come up with a more feminine touches. There's white marble all around, heated floor tiles, a glass-enclosed shower next to a hot tub. I splurged on high-end fixtures and custom finishes, such as gold and crystal accents and a mirror above the vanity that covers almost the entire wall. The window is small and unobtrusive, but it's the first thing her eyes wander to.

"You're on the third floor," I tell her. "And all windows have a security lock that can only be opened by me. Don't get any ideas."

She turns around to face me, her eyes piercing through me with passionate hate. Very good, she's playing her role perfectly.

I nod toward the toilet at the other end of the bath-room. "I thought you needed to go."

She nods, but doesn't move. Instead, she looks at me expectantly.

"I am not leaving," I tell her. "You either do it with me in the room, or not at all."

Her eyes widen in horror.

"No," she whispers. "Please, just a minute of privacy. I promise I won't—"

"No," I interrupt her. "Not an option."

"But—"

She pauses, her eyes darting back and forth between me and the toilet she so desperately needs. She bites her lower lip and averts her eyes as she walks over to the toilet, hissing curses at me in such a low whisper that I cannot perceive their meaning.

LIANA

"Why are you doing this to me?" I ask, my voice muffled by my hands as I hide my face behind them. I am so utterly ashamed, stripped of any pride as I sit on the toilet. His eyes remain trained on me as I relieve myself.

This is so humiliating, even worse than the time I was dumb enough to volunteer to perform a solo while singing for the chorus in high school. I forgot the lyrics in the middle of the song and made a gigantic fool of myself in front of the entire school, but right now, it feels like such a mundane thing. This is worse by far.

Of course, he doesn't answer my question. I try to forget that he's even there, and finish without ever lifting my eyes to look at him. Even when I walk over to the arguably fancy sink to wash my hands, I don't glance at him.

Regardless of the situation, I can't help but notice how lavish all of this is. If this hadn't been such an excruciatingly horrid experience, I could relish in the beauty of this luxurious bathroom. The light marble tiles feel warm beneath my frozen feet, and the golden fixtures on the sink appear to be made of real gold, not just painted over. There's a glass-enclosed shower cabin that is easily big enough for two people. The same goes for the jacuzzi tub right next to it.

Whoever this man is, he's not your ordinary psychopath, but a filthy rich one.

"Do you want to take a shower?" he asks, pulling me away from my stream of thoughts.

Yes, my mind cries. Yes, I want nothing more than to get rid of these uncomfortable clothes and wash away the horror of last night.

But what I want even more than that is for him to let me go.

"I want to go home," I say, standing before him with my arms crossed in front of my chest. As humiliating as the last few minutes were, the relief I feel now empowers me with a strength that I thought I had lost forever when I was caged up in that attic. I am still wearing the red coat over my business outfit. More and more, this hideous piece of clothing begins to feel like armor. This coat kept me warm, it provided the least bit of comfort I was allowed, and now I feel as if it has the power to protect me against him.

He narrows his eyes.

"You're not going home, and you know that," he says. "You're mine now."

He keeps repeating himself without ever giving me a clear reply. Maybe he's a politician and used to giving responses without ever answering a question.

Well, two can play at that game.

"I want to go home," I repeat. "I want you to let me go."

He sighs and shakes his head, worrying me as he takes a step toward me. I move away from him on instinct, but he doesn't let me gain any distance between us. His hand darts forward, catching hold of the ring attached to my collar. He pulls on it, so that I'm forced to lean forward, drawing me closer to him. He pulls me up and even closer, wrapping his other arm around me and pressing my body against his, while I choke against the strain he forces on my throat.

Fuck, he's strong. And so freaking gorgeous. How can a monster like him look like this? Like a goddamn Adonis. If I'd ever run into him on the street, I'd be intimidated by his handsome looks to no end. Just based on his looks, he's the kind of man who makes me weak in the knees.

Sadly, he's also the kind of man who drugged, kidnapped, and locked me up in a cold attic for an entire night.

"If you say that one more time," he hisses. "You'll go back in the cell, and this time, I won't let you out for a little potty time. Do you understand?"

I respond with an ached groan because he's pulling the collar with such force that it robs me of my voice. He realizes that, releasing his grasp a little so I can give him the answer he is waiting for.

The only answer that will not end in me going back into that horrible attic.

"Yes, Master," I say between gritted teeth.

"Now, let's try this again," he whispers. His tone has changed and is surprisingly soft in comparison to before. "I'm offering you something very nice here. Only a very bad girl would refuse such a generous offer. And what do bad girls get?"

"Punishment," I hiss.

I hate the way he's speaking to me. As if I was a dumb child.

"That's right," he says, smiling at me. I want to spit in his goddamn handsome face. The contrast between his physical attractiveness and the monster that possesses his soul is driving me mad.

"And what do good girls get?" he wants to know.

I hesitate, because I don't know the exact word he's looking for, and if I've learned anything from the short time we've spent together, it's that saying the right thing is of utmost importance with him.

"Treats?" I try, sighing with relief when I see him nodding.

"Correct," he says. "You were very brave right now, so I think you deserve a little treat. Wouldn't you agree?"

I assume this question is a trap, but I dare a subtle nod in response to it.

"I'm offering you a hot shower," he says. "As a treat for being such a good girl just now. Will you accept this offer?"

I'm scared to say yes, but rejecting anything he offers so generously seems like a dumb idea.

"Yes," I hear myself say. "Yes, Master, I would love that."

A smile appears on his face, a smile that I would almost call loving if it wasn't for the terrible person I know he can be.

"Good," he says, and lets go of me. "Have your shower then."

I don't know why, but I was dumb enough to believe he would leave the room for this. Of course, he doesn't. Instead, he walks over to the stool in front of the vanity and sits down, crossing his legs as he casts me an expectant look.

"You're... staying?" I ask, even though that questions is redundant, as he has already proven his intentions.

He nods, still smiling. "Of course. I am not going to miss this, my Pet."

I turn into a pillar, unable to move while our eyes are locked on each other. So this is what he is, a sexual predator. He is going to rape me.

But if that's what he is after, why hasn't he done it yet? He's strong, way stronger than me. Instead of asking me to undress last night, he could have ripped my clothes off and taken what he wanted from me. But all he did was threaten me by ripping my pantyhose. He pinned me down, and scared me, but he didn't do anything. When I didn't oblige his wishes, he simply left the room.

And now he's not lifting a finger either. He sits a few feet away from me, reveling in my struggle.

It's hard to ignore the warm tingling between my legs when I begin to undress in front of him. His eyes flicker with approval as I finally surrender to his wishes.

CHAPTER 14

JOSEPH

She reluctantly takes off her suit jacket, avoiding me with her eyes just like she did before. So this is her game then. She's playing the shy girl, the inexperienced good girl, the one who has never done anything like this before. All the other girls smiled and winked at me while they undressed in front of me for the first time. They flirted, seductively displaying their lean bodies as they tried to entice me.

It was all fine. I found some of them to be too sassy, especially when they made cheeky remarks during their striptease. But I was pleased with most of their performances.

Never as pleased as I am with hers, though.

Sweet little Ruby opts for a different kind of play. Her role differs from everyone else. And so does her body.

The more of her immaculate skin she shows me, the more I begin to doubt my own eyes. She's less curvy than I expected based on the pictures, her hair is darker and her ass smaller. Her boobs look different, too. They're round and firm, but are dropping lower than I would have expected from the silicone-filled melons I saw in her file. They look soft and natural, very alluring. Real.

She closes her eyes, grimacing as if she was in pain, as she finally takes off the last few pieces of clothing, her bra and the black lacey thong I already saw last night.

She looks different—but so damn beautiful that it's hard for me to remain patient. My cock rises to attention, growing harder with every piece of clothing she removes, playing havoc with my resolution.

I'm not going to touch her. I'm not going to do anything to her. I'm just going to watch.

She stands before me, bare ass naked and looking fucking delicious, when her eyes seek mine, asking for permission.

"Go ahead," I encourage her. "Take a hot shower, as long as you want. I have all the time in the world."

She swallows, pressing her lips together in despair.

"You're going to watch?" she asks.

I nod. "I already told you, I will."

She sighs, something that doesn't go unnoticed. With all her transgressions, she might just as well beg for punishment.

Later, I have to remind myself. Later.

I watch as she enters the glass-enclosed shower cabin and turns on the water. She turns her back to me, allowing me to watch her perfectly round ass while she welcomes the hot water as it streams down her flawless skin. The sigh she lets out speaks of so much relief and joy that it causes me to smile. She shall have her treat now, but nothing will spare her what's to come later.

She takes her time, using every single one of the expensive spa products I've laid out for her, soaping her body extensively, relishing the humid heat surrounding her.

"Shave yourself," I command her, after she's already spent a significant amount of time under the hot water.

She casts me an indignant look, and I can see the spark of revolt blossoming in her face, before she bites her lower lip and reaches for the razor.

"Take your time," I soothe her. "Do it thoroughly."

She mumbles something back at me, but her words are low enough to be drowned out by the running water.

"I want you smooth," I add to my order. "Every part of you. Every single day. Do you understand?"

I raise my voice, so she can hear me. She does hear me, but instead of giving the reply she's supposed to give, she just sneers at me for a brief moment.

Bad girl.

She follows the order precisely, moving very slowly and with caution. I can tell that she's trying to prolong her time under the shower, because there she feels safe from me. But she can't stay in there forever.

"I think you're done," I say, after so much time has passed that the entire bathroom has turned into a steam bath. "Turn off the water and get out."

She hesitates for a moment, standing with her back to me while basking in the last drops of the beloved shower. She can have this every day if she behaves. *If she behaves.*

I get up from my seat and fetch one of the big plush towels for her, while she finally turns off the water as I instructed. She doesn't open the glass door of the shower, but waits for me to do it.

"Please," she breathes when I approach her. "Please don't hurt me, Master."

Her voice is so weak, so frightened, suppressing another round of tears. It feels as if she truly fears me.

"I'm not going to hurt you," I promise. "I'm just going to dry you off. Turn around."

She sighs, her breath trembling the same as her voice and body. The makeup she wore must not have been waterproof, as most of it has disappeared, leaving only a small hint of black smudge around her blue eyes. Just like everything else, her eye color is not an ordinary blue, but underlined with hints of gray. This is the first time that I notice, now that she's standing in bright light and it's hitting her from a different angle than before.

"I'm not going to touch you," I tell her. "Just stay still."

She nods. I want to believe that her shivering is not only because of her fear for me, but because she's getting cold now that the shower is turned off.

I go down on my knees before her, something that she won't see often. It's a gesture that serves a purpose. I don't know if she's just an incredibly good actress, or if she's actually afraid of me, but in any case, I need to gain her trust. She needs to know that I stay true to my words, the good *and* the bad.

I told her that I wouldn't touch her, and I won't. When I begin to dab the water off her body, I make sure that there's no direct skin to skin contact. The towel is always between us, never exposing her to my touch, no matter if I travel along her ankles, her slim legs, her soft thighs, her alluring core, or the curves of her perfect breasts.

I can sense her relaxing more and more with every inch. Her growing trust is palpable.

"Lift your arms," I tell her, and she obeys immediately.

I finish drying her off, gently lowering her arms when I wrap the giant towel around her shoulders.

"You may wrap this around you, if you feel more comfortable," I whisper in her ear. "But you're not putting on any clothes just yet."

She doesn't give me a reply, but wraps the towel around herself, hiding her beautiful body from my hungry eyes.

"Did you enjoy that shower?" I want to know.

She nods. "Yes."

"What do good girls say?"

A frown fleets across her face. "Yes, Master."

I lift an eyebrow at her. "Almost. I just gave you a treat. Don't you think you should thank me?"

Her eyes flicker with hatred. She's brilliant. The agency really did an excellent job this time.

"Thank you, Master," she hisses. And even though her words aren't heartfelt, I let her go for now.

"You're welcome, Pet," I say. "Come with me."

I lead her by hooking my finger in the ring on her collar, wishing I had taken the leash with me so I could do this properly.

Later.

She holds on tightly to the towel wrapped around her body, her face apathetic and hard to read, as she follows me into the next room.

CHAPTER 15

LIANA

I know very little about what a person is to do in a situation like this, and I curse myself for it. There are so many warnings out there, so many self-defense classes for women, so many "how-to" videos that could have taught me some valuable tips. Tips to escape, tips to stay strong and sane, tips to outwit him so that I can create a chance to escape.

But I know nothing. I am helpless and completely at his mercy. It would be easy to escape his grip as he leads me by pulling at the collar, but where would it get me? If I started running, he would catch me within seconds. He is a strong and fit man, as far as I can tell. Fitter than me, that's for sure.

Besides, where would I even run? From what little I saw through the windows as he dragged me through the hallway, it appears that we are out in the middle of nowhere. I saw nothing but a vast and empty landscape, no other houses, no people, no cars. I have no idea how long I was passed out, but it must have been long enough for him to get me out of the city, even beyond its suburbs. I don't even know if we're still in Massachusetts, or if he took me over the border to another state.

I hold on to the towel, leaving all of my clothes behind in the bathroom, as he leads me out through a door other than the one we came through earlier. It doesn't open up to another hallway, but to a room.

A room unlike any I have ever seen before. It's a gigantic bedroom, with a massive canopy bed to my right. The bed frame is made of black steel with an elegant design and light curtains that are draped to the sides. I cannot help but notice the shackles that are attached to each of the four bed posts. This bed is designed for tying someone down.

The light gray carpet feels soft and warm beneath my naked feet, and if it wasn't for the circumstances under which I am being led in here, I could actually appreciate this beautiful room, with its high ceilings, the stucco elements gracing the white walls, and the pearl white vanity desk placed opposite the bed. There's a big mirror on top of the desk, surrounded by a row of small lights, and carved details on the frame, as well as on the desk itself. Other than those two items, there's only a dresser, featuring the same design as the vanity with a pearl white finish and marble top. There's a door right next to the vanity, but it's closed—and most likely locked.

The dark steel of the bed stands in stark contrast to the rest of the room, just as my leathery collar.

He comes to a halt and lets go of me, giving me a few seconds to take in the room. There are two big windows right in front of us, and even from afar I can tell that they are double-glassed and locked. The view is both beautiful and discouraging at the same time. The same green landscape I saw before, gorgeous but deserted.

"Don't get any ideas," he tells me. "No one will hear you, and no one will see you."

"I think I got that part," I snap at him, and as soon as I do, his hand is back on me, grabbing my upper arm and squeezing it so hard that I groan in pain.

"Don't get smart with me," he hisses. "You don't want to test me any further."

Test him? Is that what he thinks I'm doing?

We exchange a quick and angry stare before he drags me over to the bed. Panic arises in my chest as he moves me closer to the steel frame with its daunting shackles.

"You've been giving me a hard time," he says, turning me around to him and with my back to the bed. He pushes me backward, until the back of my knees meets the edge of the bed, and I involuntarily sink down to sit on it, directed by his hands on my naked shoulders.

I shut my legs, pressing my knees together firmly, but he forces one of his legs between them, nudging me to move them apart. Even with the towel still covering the most intimate part of my body, I feel utterly exposed in front of him, especially when he's not satisfied and pushes my legs even further apart.

"Look at me," he says.

I follow his order, and as I slowly raise my gaze up to him, I notice the thick bulge between his legs. He's hard, very hard from what I can tell. His suit pants stretch tightly over his erection, leaving little to the imagination.

I blush at the sight of it, hit by surprise as I realize my own arousal.

How can I possibly *like* this? How can my body betray me like this, when my mind is trying nothing but to find a way out of this horrible predicament?

Of course, he noticed my short hesitation at the sight of his hardness. I'm met with a cocky smile when our eyes meet.

"You can play with it when I allow it," he says, as if it would be the most natural thing for me to beg for his cock after what he did to me. "For now, all you have to do is listen to me, obey, just follow along, and I promise you, you won't regret it."

As if I had a choice. This is nothing but cruelty, but he speaks of it as if he's being generous with me.

I flinch when he touches my face, caressing along my left cheek before he takes my chin between his thumb and his index finger, holding me in place as I try to evade his touch.

His hands are warm and surprisingly soft. I could enjoy his touch, if I was receiving it voluntarily, but like this? I refuse to enjoy this, despite my body's insane reaction to him.

"Don't fight it," he whispers, as if he can hear my thoughts. "It'll be so much better if you don't fight it."

I want to tell him to shut up and leave me alone, but I'm too afraid. I'm too afraid of everything, of him, of myself, of that horrible attic he just freed me from. It's a perversion that I'm actually grateful. I'm grateful that he took me out of there, even though he was also the one who locked me up in there in the first place.

Stockholm Syndrome. Even I have heard about it. Is this how it starts? Am I already falling for his tricks?

He goes down on his knees, placing himself between my legs, and I'm awfully aware of my nakedness below the towel, my naked core only inches away from his face now.

He looks up at me, still holding my face by the chin, as if to make sure that I don't break eye contact.

"I'm going to make you come now," he announces, as if it was the most normal thing to say. "Drop the towel."

CHAPTER 16

LIANA

His hands are resting on my naked thighs, patiently waiting as he fixates his unyielding gaze on me. Instinct tells me to protest his command and not expose my body to him like he asked, but I'm afraid of the consequences if I don't.

"Drop the towel, Pet," he repeats. "You have to trust me."

Trust him? He is about to rape me, and he tells me to trust him? What the hell is going on inside his head? Are there two wires touching that shouldn't be?

"How can I trust you after what you have done to me?" I ask him.

He chuckles.

"Done to you?" he asks. "I just let you take a very long, hot shower. You're not very grateful."

I frown at him. It's like speaking to a wall.

"You kidnapped me," I remind him.

An angry flicker darts through his eyes, and his lips move as if he wants to say something. But he stops himself and inhales a deep breath, closing his eyes for a second before he continues speaking.

"Okay, if this is how you want to do it," he says in a low voice. "Let me phrase it this way. You either drop this towel now and let me enjoy your beautiful body, or I will lock you up in that attic again, naked."

His words feel like a dagger stabbing my heart.

"And I won't come back for you, no matter how much you cry and bang against that door," he adds. "Remember how cold it was in there? Do you really want to find out what it's like to spend an entire day and night in that room without anything to keep you warm?"

I bite my lower lip.

"You're a fucking monster," I hiss at him.

He smiles, suggesting a subtle nod. "Maybe, but you're mine now."

I'm lost. I believe him when he says that he will lock me back in that room, and that's the last thing I want to happen.

I close my eyes in defeat, slowly relaxing my clenched-up arms as I lower the towel and let it drop onto the bed sheets. There are people who say they go to their 'safe space' in their mind when they are faced with something unpleasant, like a dental procedure or a blood draw, or when other people do something horrible to them. Like rape.

I don't know where my safe space is, though. I don't know where to go when he gently pushes me back, telling me to lie down, my core bared to him. His hands trail from my shoulders down to my breasts—only cupping them for a moment, accompanied by an approving growl—before he wanders further, tracing along the sides of my upper body. It tickles and I cannot help but let out a giggle that feels entirely out of place.

"Ticklish, huh," he comments. "Good to know."

I don't respond, but just stare at the white canopy above me. The thin curtains are draped around the dark bed frame in an elegant fashion, seemingly random but with a deliberate grace. I try to focus on the elegantly swung fabric that spreads out above my head like a cloud formation, as his hands lazily travel further along my body.

His touch is surprisingly gentle, but I refuse to enjoy this. Only a sick person would find pleasure in what he's doing to me.

I suppress a moan when he places his hands on the inner side of my upper thighs and spreads my legs farther apart. His face is so close to my exposed core that I can feel his breath on my lips.

I close my eyes, preparing myself for an assault that doesn't come. He caresses the inside of my thighs, moving ever closer to my center, so close that his fingertips almost touch my soft labia, but before they do, he retreats and moves in the opposite direction toward my knee. His warm touch explores every inch of my body, going all the way down to my feet and toes, massaging my ankles and my thighs before he moves back to my knees. Then he's stroking along the outside of my upper thighs before he reaches my hips and traces along the bones that poke out as I lay on my back. I try to hold it together, but cannot help flinching and giggling as he finds the ticklish point on the side of my waist again.

He greets my sensitivity with a chuckle before he lifts his hands, only using one finger as he follows the outline of my pelvis back to my core.

But this time he doesn't stop before reaching my most sensitive area. I gasp when the tips of his fingers fondle the soft skin of my lips.

I refuse to enjoy this. My mind is set.

My body, however, turns out to be a traitor.

"Look at that," I can hear his arrogant voice as he moves farther to the inside, approaching my wet entrance. "You're practically drooling, you little slut."

Heat rushes up to my face, and I close my eyes, as if that could make any of this go away. Of course, I'm wet as hell after all this teasing. Isn't this my body's way of protecting me? I've heard that rape victims do get wet as the deed is happening because our body creates fluids no matter what. It's a mechanism of protection.

But he hasn't done anything. He's barely touching me, especially not *there*, and he has *not* been inside me. Yet.

A slick sound confirms my body's betrayal when he finally slips a finger inside my channel. I moan, still in denial that this feels good. It *can't* feel good. He's evil. This whole situation is fucked up.

He moves slowly, testing, waiting for my reaction. A hum of approval vibrates through the air when he sees me arching my back and moving my hips closer to him.

I give up. This is insane, it's sick, and it's scary. But if I have to endure it, I might as well make it as easy as possible on myself.

So what if my safe space is right *here*? In this room. With him.

"Good girl," he coos, sending another spark of plea-sure through my body. "Very good girl. Just stay like this and let go."

There's no protest. Even my mind has surrendered to my horny body. I don't even care that I let out another moan when he leans forward and I can feel his tongue circling around my wet clit. The sensation is electric, better than any man has ever made me feel. He's so gentle, so careful.

Too careful.

I want more, and I can't keep myself from verbalizing that wish.

"More," I breathe, thankful that I cannot see him right now. I would hate to see his condescending smile as he realizes my defeat.

He closes his mouth around my clit, alternating between sucking on it and drawing circles around it with his skilled tongue, while he adds another finger to spread me wider. A little bend of those fingers is all it takes for me to feel the first harbinger of an impending climax.

Why am I even surprised? He said he was going to make me come, and that's exactly what he's doing.

CHAPTER 17

JOSEPH

She explodes on my hands with such a force that it looks as if she might lose consciousness again. I know how to get a girl off, but every time I do, I'm met with the same accusing look that she's casting at me now. This face of indignation and confusion that tells me only one thing: you're not supposed to be this good.

But very few have been as responsive as Ruby. She was glistening wet before I even touched her between her legs, and she began quivering as soon as I started fingering her. Bending my finger inside of her was all it took to send her over the edge, finding that magic spot that seems to be a myth to other men, and to most women, as well. And yet it works so well.

I can feel her tension squeezing around me, her tight pussy clenching around my fingers as she's overtaken by waves of pleasure, arching and straightening her back, while her hands dig deeply into the sheets, grasping them for dear life.

Her breath only calms down slowly, and I can see a single drop of sweat traveling down the side of her left temple. I withdraw my fingers and make sure that she's watching when I lick them clean, relishing the taste of her juices. Of course, she blushes at the sight and casts me another exasperated look.

"You're sick," she breathes, but her eyes are passing right through me as she says it. Those words could be directed at herself just as much as at me.

"You're delicious," I retort, making her squirm with shame.

She tries to gather the towel around herself to cover her body and shield it from my hungry eyes, but I hold her back by grabbing her wrist.

"I didn't say you could do that, did I?"

She frowns at me.

"Of course," she whispers. "You're not done with me, are you?"

I laugh at her words.

"I won't be done with you for a long time," I say. "We're just getting started."

I let go of her wrist and get back up on my feet, now looking down at her, as she's sprawled out in front of me, completely naked except for the collar around her neck.

She looks up at me, fighting the urge to shield herself from my gaze. I can see her arms and legs twitching, moving ever so slightly, but never daring to cover herself up.

"Did you enjoy that?" I ask her. The question is redundant, but I need her to confront her pleasure. I need to see how honest she is.

She shakes her head. "No, I didn't."

I raise my eyebrows, cocking my head from one side to the other.

"I think you're lying to me," I say. "Your body is more honest than your mind."

"You tricked me," she hisses.

I laugh. "Tricked you? How?"

Little Ruby blushes, unsure what to say. She looks like a young virgin who just had her first orgasm. This lady set her mind on playing a certain character, and she sticks to it no matter what. She's so convincing at conveying her role that I would even consider giving her a raise. She's far too good to be nothing but an elaborate prostitute.

"With... that," she says, waving me off. "Whatever you did there."

She flinches when I climb on top of her, forcing her to lay back as I hover above her, placing my hands next to her pretty face as I lean down close enough for our noses to touch. She freezes, her gray-blue eyes sparkling with fear and curiosity alike, as they lock onto mine.

"I made you come," I whisper in her face. "And you loved it. Stop lying to me."

She inhales audibly, objection dancing on the tip of her tongue.

"You liked to be touched like this, you liked to be ordered around, you liked my tongue on your greedy pussy," I continue. "And you were begging for so much more, clenching around my fingers, yearning to have my big cock inside you. Weren't you?"

Her chest heaves under me as her breathing accelerates and her cheeks glow with pink heat. She slowly shakes her head, biting her lower lip as if to prevent herself from saying something stupid.

"What will you do to me now?" she asks instead of answering my question.

"You want to come again, don't you?" I ask back.

She swallows hard, not deigning me with a response.

"Well," I say, getting up from the bed. "You may have an idea of what this is going to look like, but I will explain it to you anyway. Get up from the bed."

As she follows my command, I walk over to the dresser next to the bed, opening one of the upper drawers. Everything in here, even the drawers in this dresser, can only be opened with keys that I possess. She's not supposed to have access to the toys I will be using; it's better that way. She's going to get addicted to the thrill I give her, the pain and the orgasms, but I want to own every single one of them. She's not allowed to do anything to herself and not to try anything without me present.

I retrieve what I was looking for and bring a black leather leash with me when I return to her. Much to my surprise, she's standing next to the bed, still naked, not even attempting to wrap the towel around her.

"Good girl," I say to her, even though her look suggests that she doesn't understand what I'm praising her for.

"Now, get down on your knees," I add, pointing to the floor right next to my feet. "Sit on your heels, hands on your thighs."

She pauses for a moment, giving me a look as if to say that there's no way in hell that she's obeying my words. But she doesn't need more than a raised eyebrow to be reminded of her place. She kneels in front of me, placing her hands on her thighs, but not in the way I want her to.

"Palms up," I say. "And straighten your back. Look up at me."

She sighs and even though I cannot see it, I'm sure she's rolling her eyes at me before she lifts her chin and meets my eyes.

"Better," I say. "Not good, but better. Stay like this, but open your legs for me."

She sneers at me through narrowed eyes, but obliges and moves her knees apart.

"Good," I conclude. "Remember this position. I want to see you like this every time I walk into the room, and every time I tell you to kneel. Understand?"

She nods. "Yeah."

A bolt of fury races through my chest. Is she really that forgetful, or do my words mean nothing to her?

"What have I told you to?" I snap at her. "How are you to reply to me?"

She sighs again. "Yes, Master."

"All that forgetting and sighing won't be ignored," I warn her. "You better watch yourself."

She presses her lips together, most likely to keep herself from retorting with a sassy response. Her eyes follow me as I drop down onto my knees in front of her and attach the leash to the ring on her collar.

"Every pet needs a leash," I say. "Wouldn't you agree?"

Her eyes are piercing, dazed with anger and worry. She's angry but alert at the same time, sensing my fury. She may not fear me in the same way she did when I first brought her here, but she has an idea of the beast existing inside of me. She knows I don't want to hurt her, but she knows that I will if she gives me a reason.

And she has given me plenty.

CHAPTER 18

LIANA

He's clasping the other end of the leather leash in his hand, hovering next to me like a possessive dog owner. It's humiliating and degrading, but I find myself yielding to the role more easily than I would have imagined. This role play was embedded in the crevices of my darkest fantasies, a collar, a leash, a handsome man using me for his pleasure and rewarding me with bliss in return. It's scary how much of this closely resembles the images that have been haunting me for years. Images that I tried to bring to life in my failed relationship with Luke, who only considered my fantasies to be psychotic. He said I was disgusting and sick, and I let him believe he was right.

Now here I am, coerced to be someone I always wanted to be, stripped away of everything I was in the real world outside of this gilded cage, my core still throbbing from the most intense orgasm I have ever experienced.

This could be perfect, if I knew I could go home tonight and return to my normal life.

My normal life. The life that was robbed of everything that was good in the days leading up to this terrifying event. It's a Saturday morning and I have nowhere to be, no one waiting for me, no one wondering where I am. No one will miss me until Monday, when I'm supposed to show up for work at the university. They will notice I'm gone, but I'm not sure they will be *worried* about it... definitely not worried enough to search for me.

Sadness overcomes me when I realize there really is no one else. I haven't spoken to my mother in years. She will only hear about my disappearance once the police get involved, if then. How long will that take? Days? A week? Two? Will Luke realize I've fallen off the radar? He and I haven't spoken a single word since I threw him out of the apartment nearly a week ago, and I see no reason for him to contact me at this point.

Two days, at least, maybe three, that's how long it will take until someone becomes suspicious that I'm no longer where I'm supposed to be. Will I still be here then? Will I still be alive?

"Are you hungry?" the man I'm supposed to call Master asks, jarring me away from my depressing thoughts.

I *am* hungry, but I don't want to admit it to him. Judging by the light streaming in through the window,

I'm assuming it's still early morning. I only had a light dinner before leaving the house last night. The last thing I consumed was that cheap drink at the bar last night.

"I'm thirsty," I tell him, not admitting my hunger. My thirst is far worse than my hunger.

"I imagine you are," he says. "And I'll give you some water in a minute. But food is a different story. You'll have to earn food. Do you understand?"

"Yes, Master," I say, ignoring the silly sensation of pride in regard to my obedience.

Silence stretches between us. He looks at me with a questioning face and I reciprocate the look.

"You don't want to know how?" he asks. "What it is you have to do for food?"

"I'd like to know a lot of things," I hiss back at him. "Food is the least of my concerns."

He narrows his eyes, and before I can fully grasp the meaning of his expression, he yanks on the leash, choking me and forcing me forward. I lose hold of my stance as I have to support myself with my hands on the floor. I'm coughing and gasping, caught by surprise and trying to process the pain in my throat.

I almost fall over when I try to reach for my burning throat, and he yanks the leash again, now pulling me behind him as he drags me across the room. I'm forced to follow him on all fours, humiliated and furious.

He heads for the other door, unlocking it and kicking it open. He continues dragging me behind him as he walks through into another room. The interior of this room couldn't be more different than the bedroom we were in before. The floor I'm crawling on is wooden and creaks, similar to the floor in the attic, but it's a darker color. It's painted in black, and the four walls surrounding us are painted in a deep red.

I freeze when I see a giant X-shaped piece of equipment nailed to the wall opposite the windows. I know it's meant for tying people up, submitting them to the mercy of another. The X is not the only thing that catches my attention. The entire room is filled with furniture and objects that aren't typically part of a welcoming living room, but instead belong in a torture chamber. There's a bench in the middle of the room. It looks a bit like one of those sawhorses found in the school gym, except for its black color and the shackles attached to it.

A glass cabinet at the other end of the room displays all kinds of toys and utensils, whips, cuffs, floggers, canes, and other things that I cannot identify.

He watches me as I take in the room and its trappings, an expression somewhere between horror and fascination evident on my face.

"You asked me what I'm going to do to you," he says. "This may give you an idea."

I take in the volume of toys and utensils on display in the room. I feel a small sense of relief when I don't see any knives or similar tools that might be used to kill or maim me.

"You're a sadist," I say, looking up at him with frightened eyes. "Are you going to kill me?"

He furrows his eyebrows. "Let's not go overboard."

Another yank at the leash forces me to follow him the length of the room until we reach the cross.

"Stand up," he commands.

I swallow hard, unsure whether to happy to be back on my feet, or worried about what he might do next.

CHAPTER 19

JOSEPH

I didn't like that last question. Am I going to kill her? Why would she say something like that?

She looks tense and nervous, back to the frightened young girl, the one I tried to get rid of by making her come on my fingers.

"Does this scare you?" I ask her.

She nods. "Yes."

Again, she forgets to address me properly. I'm about to lose my patience with her.

"Good," I say. "It's supposed to scare you, because this is where most of your training will take place."

She looks up at me, her eyes now filled with bewilderment. "Training?"

"Your punishment," I clarify. "Your training is ongoing, there's no physical place for it. But this is where you'll be punished."

I pull on her leash, forcing her to come closer to me. She follows the motion, grimacing in pain as the collar cuts harshly into her throat. Her breathing speeds up when I lean forward, placing my mouth so close to her ear that her wet hair dances in the current of my breath.

"I'll whip you, cane you, spank you, tie you up, and force you to come again and again," I whisper, relishing the heat that radiates from her cheeks. "And you'll love every second of it."

She doesn't have to agree or even say anything. It's all clearly written on her face when I retreat back a couple of steps to look at her. Her mouth is partly opened, as if she's about to speak, but no words escape her lips. She looks up at me, her cheeks burning red.

"What do I have to do?" she finally asks. "To get food?"

I raise my eyebrows, giving her a chance to correct herself.

And this time, she notices her mistake all on her own.

"Master," she adds. "What does my Master want from me?"

I smile at her. "Good girl."

It unnerves me that she's flinching away from my touch when I lift my hand to caress her pink cheek.

Time. She needs time, more than any of the others needed. There's no way for me to direct her behavior other than through the training methods laid out in the contract. I can't tell her to tone it down, I can't tell her to be more open to the task she signed up for, and I can't tell her to be less afraid. Maybe she's not even *acting* afraid, maybe it's the real deal. Maybe she really *is* this afraid because she didn't understand what she was really getting herself into.

"I want you to accept your first punishment," I tell her. "For the many transgressions you've incurred so far."

She bites her lower lip. "I thought the attic was my first punishment."

I smile. Touché, little Ruby.

"Yes, you're right," I agree. "That *was* your first punishment. But there have been *so* many other breaches since I let you out of there, one punishment wouldn't come close to making it right."

She furrows her eyebrows, trying to recall the mistakes I'm talking about.

"You forgot to address me properly, many times, you've talked back, you haven't answered simple questions, you've refused to follow commands," I explain. "Shall I go on?"

Ruby shakes her head, rolling her eyes at me *again*, this time in clear sight.

"And that," I say, pointing at her eyes. "Rolling your eyes at me is one of the worst offenses. If I was you, I'd cut that one out immediately."

She presses her lips together and nods. "Yes, Master."

"I'll tell you what," I add. "Since you're new, I'll be gentle. One punishment to even the score and set you back to zero. Does that sound fair?"

She hesitates, her eyes scanning the room, pausing at the glass cabinet, as she ponders her response.

"I guess so," she finally replies, adding another blow to her punishment. "What are you thinking?"

She says it as if there's any room for negotiation. Cute.

"We'll start slowly. I'll tie you up to this," I say, placing my hand on the St. Andrews Cross that we're standing next to. "And I'll spank you. I will only use my hands."

She inhales audibly, her face unreadable when she turns to look at me. Instead of saying a word, she turns her back to me and places herself the way she thinks I want to see her, spreading her legs to put her ankles into the shackles, and then doing the same with her arms.

What a good girl.

I fasten the shackles around her ankles and wrists, and take a step back to admire her. She's rather slim, but has a perfectly curvy ass that will feel soft beneath my hands. When I approach her, she flinches, burying her face against the cross and closing her eyes. I don't know if her flinching is due to the anticipation of the pain I will inflict on her, or because she cannot stand to be touched by me in general. If it's the latter, it will take a lot longer before we can proceed to actual playing. I'm not fucking a woman who doesn't want me to claim her, ever.

"Eighteen," I say. "That's how many slaps you have coming, nine on each side, and you'll count each one of them. Understand?"

"Yes, Master."

There's no hesitation this time. Her response follows as quickly and obediently as I expect it to.

I stand right next to her, my right hand caressing her pale ass cheek. It will change color once I'm done with her, maybe even leave a mark that she can enjoy for more than a few hours.

"One!" she exclaims after I release the first blow on her ass. I'm starting out slowly, only giving her a taste of what is to come, but even at the second and third strike, she's already screaming as if the pain may be too much for her to handle.

However, I know she can handle more, way more. She'll be surprised by how much she's able to withstand.

"Six!"

It's the first one that's accompanied with an actual cry. Her ass cheeks are starting to change color, now glowing in a beautiful pink. I change the location of impact ever so slightly with every fresh slap against her skin. Like an artist drawing his picture, her ass is my canvas, my hand a violent brush, awakening the blood inside her.

"Ten!"

She's trembling now, her wrist yanking against their constraints while she processes the pain. Her screams are changing, every one sings to a different melody, adding another level of pain and desperation—and lust. Her mind is drifting, moving to a place that might be new to her. It's apparent in her voice when she yells out "Thirteen!" with a groan that could be an orgasm just as easily as it could be a cry of tremendous pain.

Tiny pearls of sweat are glistening on the small of her back. Her entire body is tense, trembling under a blissful tremor, and I don't wait to unleash fourteen, fifteen and sixteen on her.

"Only two left," I tell her. "Let's make them count."

She moans an unintelligible reply. Her shrieks during the last two blows are nothing short of a beautiful song, only meant for my ears, the grand finale being her sobbing in relief as she realizes that her ordeal is over.

LIANA

W hat is this? Pain, that's for sure. I never knew
that it was possible to inflict this amount of pain
with just a hand, a simple slap on the ass, a spanking.
How something so silly can hurt this badly?

I'm feeling as if I've broken a fever. My entire body
is burning and shaking, while sweat is running down
my back. My cheeks are glowing and I feel dizzy and
confused. When I can feel the touch of his hand on my ass
again, I jerk away from him. His touch is gentle, barely
touching my tortured skin as he caresses the curve of my
ass, but the contact still sends a burning pain sizzling
through me, every nerve ending on fire.

"You did very good," he whispers in my ear, while his
hand rests softly, gently, against the heat of my skin.

I'm panting as if I'd just finished running a marathon, and I feel equally exhausted.

And *so* fucking turned on.

My mind feels foggy, thinking only of one thing. I want *more*. I want—no *need*—more of him. I need *him* inside of me.

"Look at me," his voice commands me from the left side of my body.

I obey and turn my face to him, my eyes only opened halfway when they meet his. He's fixating on me, his gaze earnest and concentrated, as if he's searching for something in my expression.

My legs spread from being tied against the cross, so it's easy for him to take advantage of my exposure, as his hand wanders lower, finding the spot between my legs that tells him everything he wants to know.

I moan when he reaches my pulsating core, gently parting my lips before he slides one finger inside. His arm is pressing against the abused skin on my ass, sending little bolts of pain through my center that mix deliciously with my arousal.

"What a slutty good girl," he whispers, his face still close to mine. "This was supposed to be a punishment. How come your pussy is drooling all over my hand right now?"

I don't know, I want to say. I really don't know.

"Did you enjoy this?" he wants to know.

I groan as he starts playing with my clit, picking up on my agitation and laying havoc with it. I know I could come like this, but I don't want to.

And I'm not sure if *he* wants me to.

"You *did* like it, didn't you?" he says, continuing his assessment. "I guess I was too nice to you."

I shake my head, still robbed of words. 'Nice' is not a word I would use for what he just did to me; it was quite the opposite, actually. The spanking hurt more than I expected. I feared every single blow more than the one before. They grew in intensity and in the level of pain. As my skin was becoming more sensitive to the torture, he only increased the impact.

I can still feel the pain oscillating through my body, but by now it has changed into a staggering throbbing that feels very similar to a slight buzz after having a few glasses of wine. It's almost pleasant.

He withdraws his hand from my center, leaving me in drenched in heat, desperate to come. He will let me come, right? He has before.

I look at him, a question clearly written on my face, but all he does is lick my juices from his fingers, relishing the taste of it. Another rush of heat spreads through my face, this time caused by embarrassment.

He goes down on his knees and unfastens the shackles around my ankles. I'm so taken by my horny vertigo, that I can't help hollowing my back for him as soon as my feet are freed and I can position them away from the cross, allowing for an invitation that was not possible before.

He chuckles next to me.

"Poor needy Pet," he comments.

I hide my face from him, ashamed at my own arousal. And he doesn't even release me from my shame by giving me what I want.

Instead, he beckons me to stand up straight, gently leading me back into position by applying a soft push on my sore behind. I cast him a questioning look when he begins to unfasten my wrists, showing no intention of taking me from behind as I expected he would. Isn't this why he kidnapped me? To fuck me? Isn't that what he said he'd do?

"You're not going to fuck me?" I blurt out, after he has released my hands and taken hold of my leash to lead me out of the room.

"Not today," he says.

"Why not?" I want to know.

He doesn't give me a response, but leads me back into the bedroom. Hope blossoms in my chest when he leads me toward the bed and attaches the leash to the black frame. He gestures for me to get on the bed, and I oblige, unsure how he wants me to position myself. I sit on my heels, the only position he has taught me so far, my hands resting on my thighs, as I cast a questioning look up at him. My naked heels feel like hot daggers piercing through the tortured skin on my ass as I sit on them.

He's standing next to the bed, shaking his head while crossing his arms in front of his chest.

"Not today," he repeats, and my heart sinks.

"Isn't that why you brought me here?" I ask. "To fuck me? To have me please you?"

He smiles.

"This *is* pleasing me," he says. "Seeing you like this is pleasing me."

I lower my eyes, averting his gaze.

"Why are you not fucking me?" I ask. My question not only comes from my greedy need for him to take me, but also because he scares me. His reluctance to do the obvious scares the hell out of me.

"Because that's not what we're doing today," he says.

I clasp my hands together, suddenly awfully aware of my own nakedness, now that the heated vertigo from before is dissipating.

"What are we going to do today, Master?" I ask, lifting my chin to look up at him.

He has his hands buried in his suit pants, again sporting a visible bulge in his crotch. This did turn him on, he wants to fuck me. A man cannot hide his need that easily.

What the hell is wrong with him?

I can ask this question all day long and not find an answer to it.

CHAPTER 21

JOSEPH

"Can I assume that you're still thirsty—and hungry?" I ask her.

She seems startled by my question, but nods. "Yes, I am."

"I'll be right back," I tell her, before I turn around to leave her room.

I can feel her eyes following me as I walk out, filled with unspoken questions.

I walk back into the bathroom to gather up her things, the clothing she was asked to drop. She's not going to wear any of them again any time soon, but her special item must be among them, and I swore to never leave a girl without her special protector. I wonder what she brought for herself. I didn't find anything when I looked through her purse, the first thing I took away from her. She had nothing but her phone and a wallet in there, neither of which she can have while she's here, as it's clearly stated in the contract.

I fold her clothes and put them in a somewhat neat pile. The only thing missing is the gigantic red fur coat. The coat was the distinctive feature that made it easy for me to find and kidnap her, and I assume it's also closely connected to the name she chose for herself. Her special item could be in one of the pockets of the coat, but as I search through them, I find nothing but a small business card.

Curious, I take the card out and hold it up to read.

Violent Delights. Ruby Red.

It's the business card issued by the agency, Violent Delights. The girls are always asked to keep their cards on them, so they can identify themselves when asked. I never know their legal names, because I don't need to. They discard their real identity as soon as they get caught up my in clutches. For thirty-nine days. I only for who they are when they are with me, and I know that person differs from the one they are in the outside world.

I take the card and put it into my pants' pocket. She no longer needs it, just like she will not need her clothes. However, I might have to ask her about her special item. I've never had to do that before, since the special item is usually obvious.

I take the pile of clothes and the coat with me, and make my way downstairs. This mansion has been in my family for two generations. I inherited it from my grandparents when they decided to move to a milder climate in Florida, and I've lived here for most of my life. I would even go as far as to say that I grew up in these lavish halls, even though my parents have never lived here with me. My father grew up here, but he left at seventeen when he was sent off to college in hopes that he would one day follow in his father's footsteps and continue the family's real estate business.

But sometimes, things don't work out as planned. Sometimes children disappoint their parents, sometimes they turn into major fuck-ups, leaving the burden for the next generation.

I grew from a bad seed, corrupted with this dark disease and vanity. Who knows what would have happened differently if I hadn't changed the course of my destiny with the help of my grandfather years ago. I don't want to think about it.

Locking up willing sex slaves every once in a while feels benign compared to the things I know I'm capable of. Yet, it's an endeavor that needs to be kept secret. Even my house staff never gets to know the full extent of what I do to these women. And every time I release another pet back to freedom, I'm met with the same look in their eyes, the same hurt, the same confusion. I break them for good. They may be wealthy and free after I'm done with them, but they're no longer the same person.

Since I sent my staff away, I will have to prepare my own food for the next few days. I usually have a personal chef on hand whenever I need him, but that's mostly for times when I'm too busy to cook for myself. These thirty-nine days are my vacation, my reprieve. I select these days carefully and set things in motion far in advance, leaving myself with more freedom and time away from the business while I have a pet at home. I can't withdraw completely and leave the business to itself for more than a month, but I can make sure that there are no major transactions, deals, meetings and contracts that need to be arranged during this time. It's just business as usual, demanding not much more of my time than a couple of hours a day.

Ruby's temporary living quarters take up most of the uppermost floor, an area that no one but me ever enters. My bedroom is right below hers, making it possible for me to hear her move around in her room, unless she's locked up in the attic as punishment. Every door upstairs locks automatically, and only I have the keys to open them. All other doors are usually open, so the cleaning staff can enter at any time. Except for one room, my office. It's right next to my bedroom, revealing too much about my sick obsession with the pet that's living upstairs. They're never free of me as long as they are here, even if I'm not physically present, but they don't know it. Cameras in several corners take note of every movement, telling me of any transgressions during my absence.

I store her clothes in my office and then continue down to the first floor. The open kitchen is connected to a wide dining area that gets used rarely for special occasions. I'm usually by myself and prefer to eat at the counter instead of sitting at the huge table all by myself. I've never had a pet down here, because it wouldn't be right. They have no place in my life outside of feeding my dark desires.

But I have cooked plenty of meals for my girls down here. I enjoy cooking, and it's gratifying to prepare a meal for someone else, someone who's giving so much of herself to me.

Ruby looked exhausted and starved, and she needs a proper breakfast to fuel her with new energy. I prepare her a good-sized portion of buttered whole grain toast, two scrambled eggs, bacon strips and half an avocado topped with some fresh fruit on the side because I know these women always ask for something fresh. She doesn't strike me as someone who eats a dish like this on a regular basis, but I'm sure she'll appreciate it now.

However, when I bring the plate up to her room, I don't find her eagerly staring at the door awaiting my arrival. Instead, she's curled up on her bed, still on her leash, and fast asleep.

She looks so peaceful, so unbelievably beautiful. I don't have the heart to wake her up, but instead I leave the plate on her nightstand, carefully placing the blanket over her naked body before I retreat, trying to make little to no sound as I close the door.

CHAPTER 22

LIANA

I wake up confused and disorientated for the third time in the last twelve hours, but this is the first time that I find myself comfortable.

I'm lying on the softest bed I've ever rested on, nestled in warm, slippery silk sheets in pastel colors and covered by a matching blanket that hugs my body like a gentle lover's arms, as soft as cashmere. Only when I try to move am I reminded that this is not an ordinary bed or an ordinary bedroom. The leather collar cuts into the skin of my throat, choking me as I try to turn my head to the side, painfully jerking the leash that's attached to the bed frame.

I have a look at the clasp and realize that I could probably unfasten it on my own, but something tells me I shouldn't. He has me chained here for a reason, and he said that I was not allowed to take the collar off. This probably goes for the leash, as well.

Luckily, the leash is long enough to give me some leeway so that I can sit up straight. The room is brightly lit, a stream of New England's brilliant sunshine breaking through the sheer curtains, immersing the room in a warm glow. I have no way of telling what time it is because there's no clock in this room either, but the gurgling growls coming from my stomach announces a dire need for food. It's been so long since I've eaten a proper meal, that I have trouble trusting my eyes when I notice the tray to my left. There's a giant plate filled with fluffy scrambled eggs, perfectly cooked bacon, buttered toast, a sliced avocado, a serving of fresh fruit salad, and a bottle of spring water. I quickly reach for the water, as my thirst overpowers my hunger by far. After emptying half of it a few greedy gulps, I turn my attention back to the food.

Did he make this for me? How come I cannot remember him bringing this in here? Was I already sleeping? And he didn't get mad at me? I remember just wanting to rest my head a little. After all that had happened this morning, I just needed a moment to rest. And the sheets were so inviting, so soft.

I don't waste any more time thinking, and instead reach for the plate so I can place it on my lap to eat. As I pick up one of the crisp bacon strips, I cannot help but laugh. This is so absurd. The whole situation, this scene.

Me, sitting in a lavishly made bed, naked, a leather collar around my neck, and my ass cheeks still burning from the beating I received earlier, digging into one of the best homemade breakfasts I've had in weeks, maybe months. I haven't been eating right since my relationship went to shit, and it only got worse after what happened to Professor Miller. This is the first time that I've been able to enjoy food in days.

Here of all places, and now of all times.

I still haven't figured any of this out, though. I don't understand why I'm here, and I don't understand why any of this is happening, a twisted dream—a fantasy— coming true in its darkest form.

Maybe that's what it is? A dream? Maybe someone drugged me while I was at that bar, slipped something in my drink when I wasn't looking?

Just as I get caught up in my paranoid stream of thoughts, the door opens and *he* walks in. He has changed his clothes and is now wearing butt-hugging black jeans and a gray cashmere sweater over a white collared shirt. His dark hair is gelled to the side, and he looks freshly shaved, baring his angular jaw. I freeze mid-bite, watching as he approaches the bed taking deliberate steps, his arms crossed in front of his chest.

"I see you're enjoying your breakfast," he says.

I lower my eyes, very aware of the fact that I'm still naked, my hair ruffled, and God knows what my face must look like with all the smeared make-up. I feel infe- rior to him in so many aspects, causing me to question if I'm even worth being kidnapped by a man like him. Couldn't he have found someone so much better than me for himself?

And why does a man like him even see the need to kidnap a random woman off the street? From the looks of it, he could have anyone, any beautiful woman he wanted, a luscious chic in a fancy dress and stiletto heels, parading her immaculate body, and perfectly dolled up to the nines to please him. Like that *Barbie doll* at the bar.

The Barbie from whom I stole that red fur coat.

What if...?

"You better finish all of it," he says, interrupting my inner ramblings.

He's sitting on the edge of the bed, casually supporting himself on his left hip as his eyes wander back and forth between me and the plate in my lap. I notice his eyes. They're not dark brown as I thought before, but rather they're hazel, a dark hazel. I've never seen eyes like his— they're not a conventionally pretty color, but seem to be as complex as the man trapped behind them.

"I will," I say. "I was starving. Thank you, Master."

It feels strange to thank him for this, after all that has happened, and all that he has done to me. His mere presence is exciting and intimating at the same time. He radiates a heated promise just as much as he does a chilling threat. I wouldn't dare not finish the breakfast he prepared for me. I'm sure there'd be another punishment attached to *that*.

I continue to eat under his watchful eyes, still troubled by questions I don't dare ask. He gives me a few moments to finish eating before he moves the tray off from my lap, telling me to present myself to him.

"What do you mean?" I ask, honestly bewildered at his request.

He rolls his eyes.

"Move the blanket away," he says. "I want to see what's mine as I talk to you."

I know he won't accept any kind of backtalk, so I just do as I'm told and move the blanket aside, exposing my naked body.

A pleased smile appears on his handsome face.

"Good girl," he says, placing his hand on my knee and slowly caressing up along the inner side of my thigh, moving toward my center.

I tense up, not ready for another round of his confusing treatment. Is abuse the right word? I'm still unsure.

"Let's clarify a few things before we go on," he begins. "You should be familiar with the basic rules, and understand the consequences of your transgressions by now, but I will summarize them for you, nonetheless."

He pauses, his eyes fixated on me to make sure he has my full attention.

"This is where you will stay, always. Unless you fail to obey and displease me. The punishment you received earlier was just a small taste of what else I have in store for you, but those punishments are only for the transgressions that happen naturally during your training, when you forget things, act clumsily, or misunderstand an order," he continues. "If, however, you openly refuse to follow an order, you'll lose your privilege to stay here."

My *privilege* to stay here? Is he fucking kidding me?

My frowning eyebrows cause him to interrupt his little lecture, casting me a warning look.

"It means you're going back to the attic," he clarifies. "For however long I decide, and it won't matter how much you scream or bang against the door. Understand?"

I nod. "Yes, Master."

"Good," he says, getting up from the bed, ready to leave.

"What do you mean by training?" I hurry to ask. "You keep saying you'll train me. For what?"

He looks at me as if the answer should be clear to me by now.

"For my pleasure," he says. "You're my pet. It's what pets are for, to be trained by their masters."

I wrinkle my eyebrows and instinctively cross my arms across my chest, closing my legs to cover my nakedness.

"Will I get my clothes back?" I ask.

He shakes his head no.

"Unless there is something specific you'd like to have?" he wants to know.

I'm confused by his question, but since he's asking, I'll answer.

"My purse, with my phone," I say. Obviously.

He laughs. "You know you can't have that."

"Why? Are you afraid I'd call the police to get me out of here?" I dare to ask. I know I'm playing with fire here, and his look only confirms that.

"You know that's not happening," he snaps at me. "So, is there anything else you need to have with you?"

I hesitate. I don't understand why he keeps pressing me on this. If he wants me to have my stuff, why not just give it to me?

"The coat," I finally say. "I want the red coat."

He sighs. "Fine."

My surprised gaze follows him as he walks toward the door. I didn't expect him to grant me *that* request.

He puts his hand on the doorknob, but before he leaves, he turns around to me one last time.

"I'll be back later," he says. "Get some rest, but don't get any ideas."

I meet his look with narrowed eyes.

"Afraid someone will hear me if I scream and bang against the door?" I ask.

His face remains stoic.

"No," he says. "No one is here. No one will hear you."

With that, he opens the door and walks out the room.

CHAPTER 23

JOSEPH

There are a lot of things that I can put on hold for thirty-nine days, but some things are out of the question. This includes the weekly phone call from my grandfather, Joseph. I'm not only named after him, but also turned out to be the son he never had, considering that my father grew to be the biggest disappointment to him imaginable.

I don't know where I would be if it wasn't for this man, so I'd never reject a call from him or my grandmother. They practically raised me, even before the untimely death of my parents. I was twelve when it happened, a boy about to start junior high school, when my father drove the car into a ravine, killing both him and my mother. They were both drunk at the time. They had been out on another binge, leaving me home alone. I was used to it, even at that young age. I didn't even notice that my parents didn't return that night, because I was already fast asleep. When the police woke me up at five in the morning by ringing the doorbell and banging on the door, I was too scared to open the door for them. It wasn't the first time that police had paid an early morning visit to our house, but this time I was afraid. I knew right away that something must have happened, and I knew right away that it must be something really bad, because they took of their hats when I finally answered the door for them. When they asked if my babysitter was home, I didn't even understand the question, and when I told them that I was by myself, they exchanged a knowing look.

It's funny how people always talk about life being unfair, about kids having unequal chances at life, about how privileged those born into rich families are. While all of that may be true, parents like mine often get overlooked. My father was privileged, sent off to the country's best business college to learn how to run the family's real estate empire built by my grandfather. But the responsibility and lack of choice that comes from being one of the privileged overwhelmed him from the beginning. He was more than just a rebel, he was angry, violent, and he hated his parents for inflicting this pressure on him. He vowed to never do it to his own son, and I can give him that. He never put any pressure on me, but that was mostly because he barely acknowledged my existence. He and my mother got married because he knocked her up when they were both still in college, and both their families pressured them to do the right thing and get married. At least they had something to connect over—a joint hate for their families, and a joint love for drugs and alcohol.

My grandparents sought legal custody of me several times, but they never succeeded.

Until my parents died.

It was as if they'd gotten another chance at raising the son they always wanted. They cared for me, they fostered me, they nurtured me, and they poured all their hopes and dreams into me.

And I didn't mind. On the contrary, I drank it all in as if I'd been dying of thirst for years. The love, the hope, the pressure, all of it was new for me, and I loved most of it.

But I was still my father's son. I've inherited some of his most loathsome traits. I'm cursed with the same rage, the same inability to control my anger when it overcomes me. Despite everything my grandparents did for me, I remained a trouble maker. Though that word may be a little too cute to describe myself.

Just like most retired elderly people, my grandparents have a pretty set schedule. They're the most predictable people I know, the only constant in my life that never changes. They call every Sunday, right after lunch, which is around 1 p.m. I don't know why they decided to make this their time to call, but that's what it is. I've not only grown accustomed to it, but made it an integral part of my week. No matter if there's a girl in the house or not, I'll be sitting in my office early Sunday afternoon, ready to pick up the phone.

It's usually my grandfather who calls as the classic patriarch of the family. But today, I hear my grandmother's voice when I answer the phone after letting it ring just one time.

"Joseph," she greets me with glee. The smile is palpable in her voice, I can practically see her face beaming in front of me. "How are you? Is it as cold up there as they say on the news?"

"It's gotten pretty chilly," I tell her. "I bet you guys don't have to worry about that down there, do you?"

"Oh, no, no," my grandmother replies. "Been more worried about the gators lately—Grandpa swears he saw one in the backyard this week!"

I laugh at her excited voice. I'm pretty sure that they don't actually have to worry about alligators in their wealthy gated community, but my grandparents like to create adventure where there's none.

I engage in a little chit-chat with her, getting reassured that both of them are doing fine, something that cannot be taken for granted at their age.

After a while, she hands the phone over to my grandfather, thus shifting the conversation to an entirely different topic. My grandparents are not afraid to be the perfect stereotype when it comes to certain things, and while my grandmother prefers to talk about the weather, my health, and random gossip about people that I don't even know, my grandfather is all about the business.

"Things going good?" he asks as soon as he's handed the phone, and I know he's not talking about me or my health, but about the business he left me in charge of.

"Yes, everything is running smoothly," I assure him. "Flipped the Lincoln properties last week, so those are finally off our hands."

"Good, good," my grandfather agrees. "Anything new on the horizon?"

"Not right now," I tell him. "I'll pick up some negotiations with those law firms in town. They have been back and forth with us for months now, and I wanted to give them some time to think things over and come up with a good proposal before I sit down with them again."

"In Boston?" he asks.

"Yes, in Boston," I say.

"Good, always good to be close to the client," he concludes.

"I know, you've taught me that," I remark.

My grandfather has taught me a lot of things, most of them business-related, of course. But even though he doesn't know it, he also taught me quite a lot about human psychology.

Years ago, that day when I went too far, when my fists destroyed lives, that was when he realized how dangerous I'd become, both to myself and others. That was the day he sat me down and told me I had to do something about it, I had to change something in my life.

"You need an outlet, son," he told me. "A hobby, sports, martial arts. Anything that will keep both your mind and your body focused. Something that captivates and controls you, something that channels all that violent energy into something less harmful, even useful."

Of course, he had no idea where I would go with his advice. I tried different things, I tried Tae kwon do, Jiu Jitsu, boxing. It helped my physique, but none of it could tame my mind.

Nothing worked as well as this.

I found my outlet in women, not in their embrace, but in their terror. They may only play a role for me, but their faces, painted with both agony and bliss are what keeps me sane.

And so far, none of them have done the job as well as Ruby.

Now as I look at her on one of the screens in my office, I can't help but feel a warm wave of gratefulness flooding my entire being.

She's tied to her bed, her naked body hidden under that red fur coat, the one thing she needs to protect herself from me. It's been two days, and I still haven't fucked her. I've never waited this long, because no one has ever made me wait this long. Ruby makes me want to take my time with her, she makes me want different things. I've spanked her, tied her down, and I've made her come again and again, and not only to gain her trust so it'll be easier to control her.

No, it's not just *that*.

I just enjoy watching her. I can't get enough of her beautiful face, her enticing body, her expressive reactions.

I can't get enough of *her*.

CHAPTER 24

LIANA

It's been seven days. Four days since I was supposed to show up at work for my last week on the job. Four days since people—someone, anyone—must have noticed that I'm gone.

I'm sitting on my bed, chained, waiting for him, wearing nothing but the lacy lingerie he provided for me—and the red coat. This is what my life has become, what *I* have become. I'm always waiting for him.

Does anyone miss me? Are they searching for me? Does my mother know? Would she even care?

After all that happened in the week leading up to my kidnapping, one could just as well suspect that I ran away, taking a leave from my normal life because I couldn't handle all the shit that had happened. It would make sense, and only a person who knew me very well would know that I'd never do such a thing. I'm responsible, organized, very predictable. There's nothing crazy about me or my life, I never overact or react in extreme ways.

Until now.

As fucked-up as this is, my life has never been as exciting as this past week with him. I'm chained, and confined to this room, locked up and pacing in my cage like a tiger, only allowed to move between the bedroom and the bathroom.

He always leaves the door to the other room locked. I've only ever been in there with him present, and every time I came back with marks on my body, my knees shaking—and my pussy dripping. He has been doing a lot of things to me that were not considered punishment, but merely part of my training. He tied me down on the bed once, using the shackles at the bed posts to fasten my hands and legs so tightly that there was absolutely no leeway for me to move. Then he forced a vibrator on my clit, taking orgasm after orgasm from me. He made me count them, just like I was told to count the spankings during my first punishment, and he made me look at him every time I came.

"Remember who is doing this to you," he kept saying. "*I'm* doing this to you. Every one of your orgasms is *mine*."

On some days, he made me come a dozen times, on other days, he tortured me with intense teasing before withdrawing the permission to come until the next day.

Those days were the worst.

He told me I wasn't allowed to touch myself when he was gone, but I did it anyway.

Once.

That day I learned that he's watching me through cameras. I should have realized it, but I didn't, and when I took a release from my body that was meant to be his, he knew.

He was so angry that I ended up in the attic again, making my worst nightmare come true. I thought he'd throw me in there without anything, making the punishment so much worse than it was during the first night. But for some reason, he allowed me to wear the red coat.

He didn't leave me in the attic for long, though. I don't know how long it was in the end, but if I had to guess, I would say it was less than three hours before he dragged me back to my bedroom. I don't know why he cut the punishment short, especially because he was still furious when he came back for me. But instead of letting me rot in that cold and dusty attic, he decided to add a few blows with a leather flogger while tying me down on the bed.

The pain was not as bad as the unfulfilled need he left me with that night. My hands and ankles were tied to the bed posts, and I winced and curled my body in agony, desperate for the release I was denied.

I think I'm beginning to understand what he means when he speaks of training. This is what he's talking about: my addiction, my need, my dependence. It's only been a week, and already I find it hard to imagine how I will ever be able to find pleasure without him.

There's only one thing that disturbs me even more than this.

He has never fucked me.

He has done everything to me, he has made me come in so many ways, touched me, teased and tortured me. He has seen me in so many states, explored every inch of my body, and uncovered a part of my soul that even I didn't know existed. He's peeling away the person I used to be, day after day, touch after touch, climax after climax.

And I haven't even seen him naked. There were times when he took me to the other room and got so worked up that he took off his shirt, treating me to a view that took away the pain in an instant. He's so ripped, his body a piece of art work, with clear-cut muscles gracing his abdomen, his tanned skin stretching over stark trenches leading down to his pelvis.

I've tried to touch him in my lusty daze, but he never allows me to. It was another kind of punishment, to lay this perfect body in front of my eyes but not allow me to play with it.

He's inked, too. But his tattoos are so unlike any I've ever seen on a man before. When I gawked at the guys lifting at the gym during my very few visits there, I would usually find words or tribal designs, sometimes animals or some kind of symmetric pattern, on their arms.

He, my Master, is sporting none of that. The tattoos covering his chest and parts of his upper arms look more like scratches or wounds, randomly placed on various places around his body. They look like marks from a fight more than a decoration. I wonder what they are all about, but I never dared ask him.

I stopped asking questions a long time ago because I've given up on ever hearing any answers. He's psychotic, a mystery—and I'm growing more and more attached to him with every day I spend in his hands, in his control.

I don't know if this was his plan all along, but he has changed me. He has brought me to a place where I find myself longing for him more than I long for the freedom from which I've been robbed.

CHAPTER 25

JOSEPH

She's waiting for me, kneeling with her thighs spread wide, her perky ass resting on her ankles, her back arched, chest forward, her head held high, and her eyes lowered. Her hands are resting palms-up on her thighs. The perfect pose of the pleasure slave.

When I close the door behind me, I can see her wince, her eyelashes fluttering as I approach her. Nothing suggests that today would be any different than the days before. She has been waiting like this for me every single day, just as I told her to. Her eyes are lowered, her body tense with anticipation, and she averts her eyes like she always does.

Nothing is different today than it was yesterday, or the day before.

Until I touch her.

When I lean forward to caress the powdered skin on her cheek, she doesn't flinch away like she did before. Instead, she leans into my touch, a soft moan escaping her lips as she welcomes me.

My heart skips a beat, realization blossoming in my chest, as I understand what this means.

She's ready.

"Look at me," I tell her.

She obediently lifts her eyes up to me. Like every day, she had no trouble following her orders to get ready for me. She's showered, shaved, smelling like a delicate flower, and her face is painted with the make-up I laid out for her. However, today she looks different than usual. I never gave her any instructions as to what I like on a woman's face, but trusted her own judgment on what would look good on her. Until now, she's opted for a subtle look, only emphasizing her natural features, and not turning her face into a mask.

Today, the black lines around her eyes are drawn out longer, adding a seductive and almost cat-like look to her face, especially as her lips are painted in blood red. She almost looks like a different person, and I'm not sure if I like it.

But I know what she's trying to tell me.

She's completely naked, only wearing the collar I gave her on the first day. I took off the leash earlier today, after bringing her breakfast, so she could eat and get ready for me. She never knows when I'll be back, but she knows that I *will* be back, and she knows that I will play with her.

Today, it seems, she has something else on her mind. She's trying to play *me*.

An entire week. It's never taken me this long to shove my cock inside the pussy that's mine. I never *had* to wait this long. With Ruby, anything else would have felt wrong.

She looks like the epitome of a sex goddess, her plush lips pouting ever so slightly while she bats her eyelashes at me.

"You look hungry," I say, as I hold her chin between my thumb and index finger, forcing her to maintain eye contact with me. "Starved for cock. Is that what you are?"

She blushes and tries to look away, but I don't let her. Her reaction calls my cock to attention. Within a moment, it's yearning to be buried inside of her. It only gets worse as I realize that today will finally be the day when that happens.

"Answer me, my pet," I tell her. "Are you hungry for my cock?"

She bites her lower lip. Killing me.

"Yes, Master," she breathes. Even the tone of her voice is different today.

I know she's not a talker. Making her say things she wouldn't say on her own is part of the game. She needs to admit to being the slut she is for me to fully enjoy her.

"Let's see what we can do about that," I say. "Put your hands behind your back, your hands touching your elbows."

"Yes, Master."

I make sure she understood the instructions before I walk over to the other room to fetch three hemp ropes from the cabinet. This should do.

She's familiar with being tied up, but I have never tied her in a proper harness before. I move her hair up to the front so it doesn't get in the way, and begin tying her up in a simple box tie, restricting her arms by fastening the rope around her upper arms, letting it cross between her breasts at the front and tying her wrists together. It's a classic tie and one I've done a thousand times before, so the motions come to me without even thinking about it. The process itself is highly erotic, serving not only to restrict her movements, but to tease her by playing with her nipples, caressing her skin in sensitive places, causing her to moan as I trace little bites along her neck.

She leans into my embrace, sighing softly every time I fasten the rope around her body. I finish tying the knot at her back, making sure that the rope doesn't cut into her skin too much anywhere.

"Does this feel good?" I ask her, still kneeling behind her, my arms placed on her shoulders.

She sighs and leans back into me. "Yes, Master."

"Good girl."

I can almost feel her heart jump at the words, and a faint smile appears on her face when I plant a kiss on her left cheek. I get up on my feet and stand before her, watching her as she gets accustomed to the feel of the rope around her chest and arms. Her back is arched, because of the strain that's put on her arms tied at her back, pushing her breasts forward. Her nipples are hard and her breasts stick out even more due to the rope cutting into her flesh around them.

"Very good girl," I praise her again, reveling in the face she makes when I begin to unfasten my belt.

Her eyes light up with excitement and she quivers, struggling against her restraints.

My rock-hard erection springs free right in front of her face, the tip already glistening with wetness. Her eyes are glued to my cock for a few moments as she takes in its size. I know I'm quite blessed in this regard, but I still enjoy seeing a girl's eyes light up with amazement and a hint of worry when she see my hard length and girth for the first time.

Ruby pulls her gaze away from my steel rod to look up at me, the sexiest pleading expression evident in her eyes.

I could give her permission and calmly tell her that she's allowed to suck on it. But I opt to remind her who's in charge here. I place my hand at the back of her head, grabbing a fist of her hair as I tilt her head back.

"Open your mouth and stick your tongue out," I command her. "Show me how hungry you are, my pet."

She grimaces in pain as I pull on her hair, but obediently opens her mouth, sticking out her tongue like a bitch in heat.

"Good girl," I praise her before shoving my length between her lips in one brute motion.

CHAPTER 26

LIANA

I'm choking on his cock, surprised by his sudden move. He's so big, but pays very little consideration to the fact that he might be too big for me. He shoves his entire length inside my mouth, until his broad tip is pressed against the back of my throat.

I gag and hack, desperate for air and fighting my gag reflex, but instead of releasing me, he pushes even further, keeping my head in place while he moves his hips forward until my lips are almost touching his pelvis.

"We'll have to work on that," he comments as I struggle for air.

He finally lets go of me, giving me only a few seconds to gasp for air before he shoves himself inside again. This time he doesn't push until he presses against the back of my throat, but shortly before that, stopping just as I start gagging again. He moves backward. Slowly. Allowing me to properly wrap my lips around his member and play along his shaft as he continues to move back and forth in a deliberate manner.

I can't balance on my own with my arms tied up like this. I'm completely at his mercy, balancing only with the help of my weak core muscles, depending on his guidance. His grip around my hair loosens, allowing me to gain some control over my own movements.

He was already hard when I began sucking him, but I can feel him growing even more solid between my lips. I'm filled with pride and accomplishment when he lets out a deep groan of pleasure, throwing his head back, losing sight of me, but never letting go of my head. Even now, as I please him to the best of my ability, he's the one who's in control.

Just as I'm beginning to feel as if I might be winning over some of that control, he stops me mid-motion, holding me back by my hair and taking a step back before he leans over, his face right in front of mine when he fixes me with an intense stare. I'm panting, desperately trying to fill my lungs with air, while saliva is running down the side of my face.

"I need to fuck you," he hisses, moving his face so close to mine that our noses are touching.

It's now that I'm made aware of something else that's been missing between us.

A kiss.

We have never properly kissed.

I lean forward, certain that this will be the time to change that, but he has other plans.

He jumps up, forcing me to follow him by dragging me up on my feet. I stagger like a newborn deer, struggling to maintain my balance without being able to move my arms.

My scalp hurts from all the hair pulling, and I sigh in relief when he finally lets go of me, instead hooking his finger into the ring on my collar to lead me over to the bed.

"On your back," he says, much to my surprise.

I climb up on the sheets, even more clumsy than usual, as I try to lay down without having the support of my arms. He notices my struggle and helps by grabbing my shoulders and slowly lowering me down to the mattress.

"Lift your legs and bend your knees," he orders next.

I'm trembling with need, dizzy with anticipation, while I position myself the way he asked me to, watching him with curious eyes while he throws another bundle of rope next to me on the sheets. Then he finishes undressing himself.

Finally.

I can't take my eyes off of him as he slowly removes one piece of clothing after another. His hard cock is glistening with my saliva, jutting out with its impressive length and delicious girth. I can't wait to feel him inside of me.

It's the first time for me to see him naked, allowed to see him in all his tanned glory. The strange ink stretches over his muscular arms when he climbs onto the bed, grabbing the rope in the process. It's easy to tell that he has done this sort of thing a lot of times before. He starts on my left leg, pushing it until it's fully bent at the knee, before he starts wrapping the rope around it, fastening it just below my knee and adding another knot just above my ankle.

I watch him, turned on and fascinated at the same time. Even after an entire week as his captive, I still struggle to place the fact that it took so long for this to happen, so I could have my darkest fantasies realized.

He moves on to my other leg, deliberately letting the rope caress over my wet center. The rough material prickles against my sensitive skin, and I see him grinning as I moan in bliss.

"Frog-tie is what they call this," he says as he fastens the last knot around my other leg. "But I think fuck-tie is more appropriate. Wouldn't you agree, Pet?"

I'm sprawled out in front of him, my legs tied and spread apart, rendered immobile by his rope skills. Before I can give him a reply, he moves his hand between my legs, casting me a mischievous smile when he finds the proof of my arousal.

"So wet for me," he whispers. "What a perfect little pet you are."

I groan a desperate response while he plays with my clit, threatening to make me come before I can feel him inside me.

"Please," I hear myself plead. "*Please*, fuck me."

He hums in approval. "Oh, I will."

My heart jumps when he reaches over to the night stand next to my bed, opening the first drawer to fetch a condom. I know that they've been in there all this time, and I've been waiting for him to open that damn drawer for so long.

I feel so adrift and helpless before him, and it's this understanding of being at his mercy that fuels my heated need for him. I've wanted to feel this way, and despite the frightening reality of these circumstances, I cannot help but yearn for the final step. For him.

He rolls the condom over his hard length in no time, teasing me by placing his head at my wet entrance with no apparent intention to move any further. He casts me a dark smile, full of promise and the knowledge that he has won.

I don't care. I don't care if he thinks he has me right where he wanted me all along. All I care for is my own pleasure, my own needs that still don't stand fulfilled. I tried to shift myself closer to him, but my legs are tied so tightly that it's hard for me to move across the sheets, especially since I can't do anything with my arms.

"Please," I beg, looking up at him, his tip already parting my lips. "Fuck me, Master."

It's what he has been waiting for, the magic word, the appropriate way to address him, especially when uttering a greedy wish.

He leans forward, his muscular chest hovering over me, while he parts me with his enormous girth, shoving his cock into my hungry core with sensual deliberation. I moan, taking him inch for inch, until his pelvis is pressed against my center, his entire length filling me like no one has before.

Again, his eyes are fixated on my face, reading every little reaction as he takes me for the first time. He stays in place for a few moments, watching me squirm beneath him, breathing rapidly as I accommodate him inside me.

His hands find their way to my bound thighs, spreading my legs apart as far as possible before he starts pounding me with a sudden savagery that takes my breath away. I shriek in surprise, but soon my cries turn into conflicting outbursts of ecstasy and pain as the rope cuts into my skin as he fucks me like I've never been fucked before.

This is raw, violent fucking that lacks the fear of consequences. We have nothing to lose and nothing to prove to each other. When he grabs me by the hip, slightly elevating me from the sheets, I feel nothing but the pleasure his rough pounding sends through my body in strong waves.

I don't worry about looking pretty for him, because I know he's mesmerized by me either way. There's something in his eyes when he looks at me, a mysterious spark that speaks of the sick devotion he has for the woman he robbed and calls his pet.

His face is lined with exertion and lust, drops of sweat running down his temples while he continues to slam into me like a wild beast. He takes what he wants from me, and I can tell that the wait has been long for him, too. His vicious handling of my body speaks of a desperate need, just as my cries of rapture do. I can only let it happen, wrapped up in hot knowledge that I'm his possession, his pet, his biggest pleasure.

A yelp of surprise escapes my mouth when he picks me up by the hips, turning me around as if I weigh nothing, temporarily withdrawing his cock from me. Even this short moment without him is enough to make me realize how much I crave feeling him inside me.

I groan with desperation, instinctively hollowing my back, begging to feel him. His hands reach for the knots at my back, tightening the rope around my chest as he pulls on it while shoving his cock back inside. I'm balancing on my knees, the rope cutting into the flesh on my legs, as I try to stretch my legs despite the restraints. It's as if there are a thousand needles, prickling all over my body, intensifying each sensation he's inflicting on me.

He keeps hold of the rope around my upper body with one hand, but the other moves between my legs, finding the spot just above my entrance. I groan when a sharp thrill bolts through my core, as he begins playing with my slick clit.

I want to warn him, tell him that I might come any moment, but my face is shoved into the sheets, suffocating every potential verbalization of my thoughts.

He wouldn't mind, anyway, it seems. His motions accelerate, torturing my body to the edge of release.

"Come!" I hear his voice behind me. "Come on my cock, my pet."

Even within the short time of seven days, my body has learned to obey his command. The groan I let out when an explosive release takes hold of me seems to come from far away, from a different person even. I bathe in a pool of ecstasy, a delight that is so voracious, it almost renders me unconscious.

Just as my climax starts to recede with its last, violent waves, I can feel him throbbing inside me, joining my elation just before it's fading.

I don't think I ever came this hard, this long. I'm physically and mentally exhausted, panting so heavily that I'm close to hyperventilating.

He turns me over onto my back, my center still pulsating with the aftermath of our joint pleasure, when he lowers himself over my trembling body, placing his elbows next to my head before he leans in for the kiss I was denied before. It's a greedy kiss, his tongue forcing its way into my mouth, as if we're just beginning our play. I reciprocate his longing, relishing the passionate embrace of our lips.

Our eyes meet when he stops our kiss, drops of sweat running down his handsome face as he moves a wet strand of hair out of my face, looking at me like he never has before.

"Ruby," he breathes. "That was insane."

CHAPTER 27

JOSEPH

Her face freezes. She looks at me with an aghast expression, her breath stopping for a moment before she gathers herself enough to speak.

"What did you just call me?" she asks.

Fuck.

Never call the girl by her name. Never.

I've been so mad at her for not sticking to the rules of our contract in the beginning, and now I'm the one who breaches it in the most pathetic way possible.

She's my whore. My pet. My toy. As far as I'm concerned, she has no name, and she's never to be addressed with any name I might have been given. This has never been a problem before.

Why now? Why did I just call her by her name? Or rather, the name she uses for her agency listing. The only name I've ever been told.

It fucks with our deal, and I damn well know that. The way she's looking at me now says it all. She's confused and alarmed, because she knows that I vowed to never address her as anything but 'my pet.' It was clearly stated in our contract what she is to me.

"Nothing," I say, moving away from her.

I jump down from the bed, leaving her tied and helpless, with her bent legs still spread apart, looking fucking delicious. Normally, I would take her with me, feeling her up and possibly fucking her against the tiles while the warm water washes our sweat away. But right now I just need to get out of her sight, pretending that my transgression never happened.

Her eyes follow me as I flee to the bathroom, hastily closing the door behind me. I hop into the shower, soaping myself in angry haste, as if I'm trying to wash my mistake away.

How could this happen? Everything was going fine, great actually, before that dumb mishap slipped my tongue.

It was more than great, though. I knew the built-up anticipation would lead to an outburst of unmatched degree when I finally fucked her, but I didn't expect it to be like this. This fantastic. Mind-robbing. Violent.

I lost myself with her. I know I was rough beyond measure. Fucking her awoke the beast inside of me, the wild creature I've been hiding for so long. If I hadn't spent so much time learning to control the monster inside me, she could have been in actual danger.

But of course, she isn't. I could never hurt her for real, or take anything from her that she isn't willing to give. It's the whole reason behind my patience.

My concern for her reminds me that she's still tied up and unable to move. I turn off the water and quickly wrap a towel around my waist, before heading back to the bedroom, water dropping down my skin as I approach the bed to save her.

She's lying on her side, her legs close and squirming against her restraints, while she casts a pained grimace at me.

"I'm sorry," I tell her, gently pushing her onto her back, so I can untie her legs.

"It's okay," she whispers, her voice weak and empty.

"No, it's not okay," I say. "I shouldn't have left you here like this. Your Master made a mistake."

She looks at me, her expression lined with disbelief, as I admitted to my mistake.

"Will you accept my apology?" I ask her.

I have unfastened the knots on one leg, but hold it in its bent position, only slowly allowing her to stretch it, so the blood flow can resume normally. A sigh of relief escapes her when she's finally able to move her leg freely.

"Yes," she breathes. "Of course."

"Good," I say. "It won't happen again."

I free her other leg and let her stretch for a few moments, watching as she turns her ankles in circles, expanding her legs on the sheets as their color changes back to normal. The frog-tie is not as tough on the blood circulation as other knots can be, but my knots have been tight and she has struggled against the restraints, pushing herself to the limit while I had my way with her.

I help her to sit up, turning her back to me so I can unfasten her arms, as well. The box-tie must have been even tougher for her than the tie around her legs. I can tell by the marks the rope leaves on her delicate skin—and by her moans as she's finally freed.

She observes her skin, tracing along the red lines the hemp strings left on her, while I take up the rope. The smile on her face is the most beautiful expression I can think of. It's a smile underlined with satisfaction and pride, the kind of pride only a submissive knows. The marks are telltales of her struggle, and a reminder that she's capable of not only overcoming the pain that's associated with it, but also taking pleasure from it.

"Does it hurt?" I ask.

She shakes her head.

"No, not really," she says, sounding almost disappointed. "It's beautiful, though."

"I agree," I say. "Nothing prettier than marks on a woman after an intense play session."

She blushes as she looks up to me. Our eyes lock onto each other for a few moments, silence filled with unspoken questions stretching between us. I know she hasn't forgotten, and neither have I. I was hoping that she'd be smart enough to refrain from pointing out my other mistake again, but it turns out she just waited for the right moment to go back to it.

"Why did you call me Ruby earlier?" she wants to know, shifting over to the headboard and leaning against the cushions with her legs pulled close to her body.

I cast her a dark look.

"I'm sorry," I retort. "I shouldn't have done that. This is another thing that won't happen again."

She looks at me as if that reply confuses her even more.

"But... why?" she presses. "Why Ruby?"

Now, I'm the one who's confused. She knows very damn well why I would call her Ruby. Ruby Red. That's the name written on her business card, the name she was listed under at the agency. She must be aware of the fact that I know that name. Why is she so surprised?

"It was a mistake," I repeat. "You're my pet, and I'll never address you any other way again."

"Okay."

She looks at me as if she's trying to solve a puzzle, still in the dark about the meaning behind my mistake.

There is no meaning. Nothing to solve, nothing to understand. There can't be.

"Are you hungry?" I ask, diverting from the subject.

She hesitates for a moment, before she nods. "Yes, I am."

"I'll bring you something up," I say, gathering my clothes, before I flee from her room.

CHAPTER 28

LIANA

I always have to smile when he brings me a sandwich. Somehow, that's such a typical man-thing to do. Not that the cooked food he's been bringing me has ever been bad, but I'd still say that sandwiches are where he really excels.

Today, he brings me a roasted chicken breast sandwich with avocado and crisp bacon strips, making it a rather heavy and savory variation. The smell of it almost lets me forget about the confusion he caused earlier.

I need to know why he called me Ruby. Was it a simple mistake because he just assumes that this must be my name based on the business card he took from the coat? Or is there more to it?

I took the time to take a shower and freshen up, while he was downstairs preparing my food. He's just coming through the door when I walk through the bathroom door, instantly dropping down on my knees as I see him and taking my position.

"Good girl," he praises.

I thought he'd tell me to get back on my feet right away, but instead he places the tray with the sandwich right in front of me on the carpet, beckoning me to eat right where I am.

Just like a pet.

It's not the first time that he makes me eat like this, but I still don't enjoy the humiliation that comes with it. I know he only does it to remind me of my place, but nevertheless, I'm not forbidden to speak.

"Ruby is not my name, you know," I say, before I take the first bite of the delicious sandwich he brought me.

He's sitting on the edge of the bed, watching me while he finishes taking up the rope. His eyes flicker with anger when he looks at me.

"You're my pet," he says. "Nothing else."

I sigh. Something that doesn't go by him unnoticed. He casts me a warning look.

"Yes, sure," I say. "But, I mean, it's really not my name. My name is Liana Doy—"

"It doesn't matter!" he barks at me. "You're my pet. There's no need for names, real or not."

I wince at his loud voice, frightened by his sudden outburst, and continue to eat my sandwich, hunching my shoulders inward like a scared animal.

Why does it anger him so much when I talk about these things? It's like he's trying to block out that I'm a human being, a person with a name and a life.

Maybe this is my way out? If I make him confront all those things, the fact that he robbed a real person out of her life.

A life I don't particularly miss. But that's a minor detail that shouldn't matter to him.

"It's not even my fake name," I add.

He looks at me, a silent question flickering in his eyes.

"Ruby, I mean," I clarify. "I've never used that name. I'm Liana. Always."

It's as if an icy wind just traveled across the room, erasing all life and with it all noise from our environment. He stares at me, his expression frozen in angry confusion.

"Stop it," he says, his voice tense. "Stop breaching. We have a deal."

I reciprocate his gaze, seemingly calm from the outside, while my heart feels as if it's about to burst with fear.

A deal? What is he talking about? When on Earth did we ever make a deal with each other? He acts as if I'm her on my own volition, with perfect knowledge about the scope and rules of this—whatever *this* is.

Wait. Does this mean he thinks he's talking to someone who *does* know what's going on? Someone else but me?

"Do you think I'm Ruby?" I ask him. "Because I'm not."

Something in his expression changes. He no longer looks merely angry and confused. There's something else in his demeanor, something I've never seen on him before.

Fear.

"Shut up," he snaps at me. "Finish your goddamn sandwich."

"Did you find that name on the card you took?" I ask. "The card that was in the coat's pocket?"

He glares at me, his fists clenching around the rope.

"If you don't shut up right this second," he hisses. "You're going back to the attic. All night. Understand?"

We freeze in an angry stare contest. I know I can't get into any trouble as long as I keep my mouth shut, but I'm not done asking questions. I'm getting somewhere with this. I'm getting under his skin, which means that I'm moving in the right direction. There's something there, something he's terrified of.

What if he made another mistake? A mistake so big that it could destroy him?

"Do you understand?" he presses, locking me down with his intense eyes.

He's already in the process of getting up from the bed. If I don't give him the reply he seeks, he will drag me over to that horrible room in no time, leaving the half-eaten sandwich and the luxury of my gilded cage out of reach for an entire night.

Is it worth risking? Is there anything I can draw from him at this point that would make this sacrifice worth it?

No. I decide that it is not.

"Yes, Master," I reply, obediently lowering my eyes as I finish eating my sandwich.

I think I may know enough to understand what's going on here.

CHAPTER 29

LIANA

Things have changed since that day he finally decided to fuck me. Our whole dynamic has shifted now that I believe I understand what is really happening here.

He made a mistake when he grabbed me off the street. He doesn't just think that my name is Ruby because it's written on the business card he found in my coat.

He thinks I'm Ruby because *that*'s the woman he was looking for. The woman whose coat I was wearing at the time when he took me. The Barbie doll from the bar. She looked like an escort to me, and by now I'm pretty sure that she actually was.

And he bought her. The deal he keeps talking about, all the times he acted as if I should know things that I didn't know. He thought he was talking to the escort he hired to do all this. An escort to live out his perverted fantasy. The fantasy of kidnapping a woman and making her his sexual slave.

None of this is real. We are playing a very elaborate form of role play. That is why he's given me so little explanation and that is why he kept complaining about me making so many transgressions in the beginning. I had no idea what was going on, but he expected me to.

Now I'm in the know. I finally understand how I ended up here. In a way, I brought this upon myself by stealing that woman's coat. If I hadn't done that, he never would have grabbed me. It was her identifying mark, the one feature that helped him find her, and the only item of clothing I was allowed to keep.

A significant amount of power has been handed over to me now that I know.

Yet, I'm still here. Naked, curled up in the soft sheets he lets me sleep in, with a collar around my neck that hasn't been taken off in eleven days.

Why am I still here?

Why can I not bring myself to tell him? He would probably let me go. He might even pay me to keep my mouth shut because he can get in serious legal trouble for what he did.

I could even blackmail him.

At least then I wouldn't have to worry about money. He must be loaded if he can afford all of this, this house, the lavish interior, his tailored suits, all the expensive lingerie he makes me wear, or just the plain fact that he can buy women to serve as sex slaves for days and weeks. I have no idea how long he intends to keep me here.

I could ask him to let me go, and only promise to keep my mouth shut if he paid me an enormous sum of money. Something that would last me for a few months, maybe even a year, until I get my feet back under me.

Because what kind of life will I be returning to? I've lost everything, my arguably idiotic boyfriend, my job, my safe haven. There's nothing waiting for me except an empty apartment, an uncertain future, and a funeral I don't really want to go to. It pains me not to be able to bid goodbye to Professor Miller, but I know that the funeral would be a terribly crowded affair. I may have been his right-hand for more than a year, but no one really knows me there, especially when it comes to his family. Maybe I would even be in the way.

It doesn't matter anyway because I'm not going. I can't go. I cannot even leave this room without his permission.

But what troubles me most is that I don't *want* to leave.

Figuring this all out is not the only thing that has changed since that fateful day we fucked for the first time. *Everything* has changed. The way I see him has changed. He's no longer a handsome but terrifying kidnapper who scares the hell out of me, but so much more. I feel weirdly close to him, attached even. I know that they have a word for this phenomenon, but I can't help experiencing it nonetheless. Now that I know who he thinks I am, I cannot help but feel differently toward him and what he has been doing to me. He's not a criminal, just a wealthy man with a dark and twisted need.

And he's so good at expressing his need. There have been many days where I felt like I was the one drawing more pleasure from this than he was. I practically had to beg him and show him with every fiber of my being how much I needed him to fuck me, until he finally did. He gives more than he takes, but insists that my orgasms all belong to him.

In a way, I can't believe how lucky I am to be on the receiving end of his dark desires.

It's still early morning, and I'm waiting for him to come unleash me from the bed, the first ritual of the day. I don't know if he has a set time when he shows up in my room because I still don't have access to a clock. But I've grown so used to all of this that I usually find myself awake a few minutes before I can hear his steps approaching. It's always enough time to fix my hair and take my position to greet him. The leash is long enough for me to leave the bed, but I usually stay on the sheets. He doesn't seem to care whether I kneel for him on the floor or on the bed.

Even our morning ritual has changed. He no longer greets me by stroking along my cheek after he first sets foot in the room. He's doing something else now.

Every day and every moment with him starts with a kiss.

Kisses were never part of the routine during our first week together, but they are so integral now that it would feel like a punishment if he took them away from me.

I love his kisses. Unlike his rough hand, they are soft and gentle, stirring something inside me every time our lips meet, a tingling that reaches all the way to my throbbing core. I always want more, and my body gets ready in anticipation, knowing that there will be more. Every day.

The days with him have become less frightening, but not less exciting. They are predictable as much as they are rich in variety. He's asking more things of me, expecting my obedience with all kinds of tasks and commands. I've become better at obeying him, and I've grown to like complying with this obedience. Hearing him praise me as a good girl and seeing him smile in that proud and complacent way, pleases me more than I ever thought possible.

But I've also become better at playing his game. I always knew that I have a suppressed desire to receive all these things, the punishments and pain, as well as the simple bliss of intense release. Agony can be more than a flavor enhancer. It's closer to a drug.

I resist and defy some of his commands by choice, just to see what he will do if I don't go along right away. I never let it go as far as getting locked up in the attic, because that's not the kind of punishment I seek.

I want to feel leather and rope on my skin. I want the breathtaking sensation of a whip cutting into my flesh. I yearn for the vertigo of throbbing after pain.

And now I'm here, in a place where I can try all of these things, with a gorgeous and troubled man. A man who no longer scares and confuses me.

I will keep my mouth shut. Only for a while longer. The last few days have been closer to a dream than a nightmare. It would feel wrong to run away now.

I jump up when I hear his steps approaching the room. He's here. It's time to get ready for another day with my Master.

CHAPTER 30

JOSEPH

She's kneeling on the bed, her hands placed on her thighs, her chin lifted, but her eyes lowered. A faint smile flickers across her face when I come closer.

No flinching, no shying away from my touch. Instead, she leans in for the kiss she knows is coming, yearning for me just as I yearn for her. Our lips meet and I close my eyes for the first few seconds we will spend together today. It will be a short day, at least in regard to the time that will be spent with her. I have to drive up to the city, even though I hate doing so when I have a girl here. But there's no way around it. I'm needed. Even my grandfather called to make sure that I would be present at this board meeting. It would only raise suspicion if I didn't show up, so I have to steal these hours away from her.

But I will make the time we have together count.

She has shown that she's different from all the others since the very beginning. She broke rules left and right, she pissed me off with her confusion and her dumb questions, her all too real terror, and her way too serious defiance. Lately, all of that has changed. She's going through the same process I see all of them go through, but her transformation is stronger, the contrast so stark that it almost scares me. She's adapting to the rules, no longer breaking them, but testing them, to tease out a reaction from me. It's exactly what she's supposed to be doing.

Now I'm the one who's breaking the rules.

No kissing. It's stated in the contract, and I've repeatedly told myself that this is off limits. Kissing is for lovers, not for a Master and his paid pet.

Of course, this one is easy to overstep. I've done it before, in the heat of the moment. But I've never enjoyed it as much as I am with her, and I've never made it part of a ritual.

I can't lose myself. I can't lose control. This is a slippery slope, and I know I'm only getting started. Today, I'm willing to go even further than I did before. I'm jumping in with my eyes open, risking more than just our contract.

Yet, I will do it. The thought of following through excites me too much to neglect this wish. I have to see what it's like. I want to see how far I can push things without losing myself too much.

Her eyes find mine when I stop our kiss, their gray-blue depths piercing through me with understanding. Despite her helpless behavior in the beginning, I cannot help but see the intelligence that radiates behind her eyes. She's smart. She gets me.

That's why she's so dangerous.

"Good morning, my pet," I whisper.

She's never allowed to be the first one to speak, and her first words are always the same.

"Good morning, Master," she says, her voice so soft that it kills me.

"Did you sleep well?" I ask her.

"Well enough," is her reply. She always says something along those lines, and I never follow up with a question.

"Let's have a shower," I tell her, unhooking the leash from her collar. She can remove it on her own because she's still wearing a training collar, but she never has. I told her she wasn't supposed to do it on her own. It was the first command she obeyed without having to be reminded several times.

"Together?" she asks as I lead her to the bathroom, pulling her by the ring at the front of her collar.

"Yes," I say as we walk through the door. "Together."

She watches as I take off my clothes, her eyes wandering along the lines of my tattoos. I know she has questions about them that she doesn't dare ask. Too often I have ordered her to be quiet when she started poking at things I wasn't comfortable talking about. The tattoos are part of that, and she seems to sense it. They are reminders of a past that I would like to forget, a past that I've put behind me. They remind me of the pain I caused and the lives I destroyed when I lost control over myself. The black ink adorns my skin like a curse.

She's shy every time we do something new, and today is no different.

"Turn on the water," I command her, mainly to stop her from gawking at me. It's flattering, but unsettling at the same time.

She turns around, deliberately hollowing her back and stretching her legs to give me the best view of her round ass. It works like a charm. When I lose the last item of clothing to follow her under the hot shower, I'm hard and ready, my cock yearning for the body that's mine for twenty-eight more days.

She squeals and smiles at me when my length pokes her in the small of her back as I join her under the welcoming water. My hands are on her wet body in an instant, following the outline of her narrow shoulders, traveling down her arms, grabbing her wrists to keep her eager hands in place. She has turned into a cock-hungry slut, hardly able to keep her hands to herself every time she sees my hardness. For the past four days, she has been getting fucked every single day, at least once, but her hunger for me only grows, just like mine for her.

"No hands," I tell her, leaning in closer so she can hear me over the running water. "Just your lips, my pet."

Even in the hot steam of the shower, I can see her cheeks blushing, while she lowers herself down to her knees. Her eyes never leave mine, even when she bends forward, placing her hands on her thighs so tightly as if they were glued to her skin so she isn't tempted to use them. I groan when she takes me between her pouty lips, her tongue gliding along the lower side of my shaft as she swallows me down. The pouring water is playing havoc with her breathing, making it hard for her to take my length without catching her own breath. She's trying so hard to take in all of me, but fails at it every time. When she withdraws to gather her breath, she casts me an apologetic smile. I pet her head.

"You're doing excellent, my pet," I praise her, and she rewards me with the cutest smile I've ever seen on a woman's face.

Her lips are wrapped around my cock again within moments, her head moving back and forth as she drives me closer to insanity. She stops for a moment, sucking on my length so strongly that it almost hurts, creating a vacuum with her mouth that allows her to play along my shaft with her tongue. The feeling is sublime.

"Fuck, who taught you that?" I ask her, out of breath with pleasure.

She sucks and then retreats, kissing and licking the tip of my hard cock while she bats her eyelashes up at me.

"My Master," she says, smiling at me seductively.

"Get up," I tell her. "Now!"

Her eyes rest on my length for one more moment, painted with a hint of disappointment as she slowly rises to her feet.

I pull her closer, my hands cupping her full ass, while I press her core dangerously close against my erection. Shit, I'm going to lose it if I can't fuck her now, bare, just like this.

Never fuck a whore bare. Never.

But she's more than a whore. She's not like the others. And I know the girls of my agency are safe and clean because they have to get tested before entering my home.

"Are you on birth control?" I reassure myself, my eyes locking on the gray-blue depth of hers.

She's breathing erratically, suffering in heated need just as I am.

"Yes," she replies, her eyes so dazed with lust that I pray to God I can trust her. "The depo shot, I just got one about a month ago."

"Good," I say, claiming another kiss from her while pushing my pelvis against her cunt. "Because I need to feel you. All of you. I need to fuck you bare."

She doesn't say anything in reply, but wraps one of her legs around me, shifting her hip so that my glistening tip is teasing her entrance.

I don't hesitate another moment and buckle my hips forward, stretching her with my rock-hard girth while lifting her up, pressing her slim back against the wall. She wraps both of her legs around my waist, supporting herself as good as she can while I fuck her like a wild beast, consuming her bare for the very first time.

She moans and yelps, her cries partly drowning in the steaming water that's running down on us. Her muscles tense around me, as if she was trying to hold on to me. The pressure almost sends me over the edge way too soon.

"I'm going to come inside you," I tell her.

A smile scurries across her face and her muscles tighten anew, forcing a release out of me that I wasn't yet ready for. I explode inside of her, filling her with my cum, as violent waves of pleasure grip my body. But even in the midst of my rapture, I never lose our stance, I never let go of her, holding her safe and as closely as possible during the highest moments of pleasure.

CHAPTER 31

LIANA

He tenses up, his hands clawing into me with such ferocity that it hurts, his cock throbbing incessantly inside me. I'm trying to hold on to him, relishing the warm sensation of his release as it coats me inside. This is the first time he didn't make me come first, but I'm confident that he won't leave me unsatisfied.

He doesn't let go of me. Instead he buries his sweating face against my shoulder and wraps his arms protectively around me, squeezing me so hard it takes my breath away.

"Master," I utter, suffocated by the sheer intensity of his embrace. "I can't breathe."

His grip loosens instantly, and he supports my body as my legs slowly find their way back to the tiles. He's breathing heavily, his dark hazel eyes shimmering with a spark I haven't seen before. The water is still running, surrounding us in a hot and comforting cloud of steam.

"Are you okay?" I ask. "You look—"

"Yes, fine," he interrupts.

It's as if my question brought him crashing back to reality, reminding him of who he is and what he's to do next. There was a moment during which he wasn't the same man who brought me here, the man with the stone-cold exterior. I could feel the shift in his embrace.

"Finish getting ready," he tells me. "I'll be back."

He puts some distance between us by taking a step back, rinsing himself one last time before leaving me alone in the shower. He snatches a towel on his way out of the shower, quickly wrapping it around his buff waist before shutting the bathroom door behind him after he leaves.

My eyes stay locked on the door for a few more moments before I can pull my attention away. I finish showering and then do as he asked, getting myself ready for him, as I do every single day. By the time he returns, I'm sitting on the floor of my room, entrenched in a fresh and flowery smell, my body silky smooth and slathered in lotion, my hair put up in a simple up-do, and my face masked in a subtle layer of make-up. I felt a little chilly, so I covered up the white set of lingerie I'm wearing for him with the red fur coat. I must look like a naughty version of a female Santa, but I don't care. He has never gotten mad about me wearing the coat for some reason, even though it hides my body from him, which is something he appears to hate more than anything.

He's dressed to the nines when he returns, wearing a navy blue suit with a matching slim tie and a crisply ironed white shirt. His hair is slicked and combed to the side, looking particularly handsome today, but he hasn't shaved. The stubble around his angular jaw is darker than it has been on other occasions, giving him a more mature look.

I realize too late that I'm staring at him, instead of lowering my eyes in that coy manner he wants. But he doesn't get mad.

"Look at you, drooling all over your Master," he says, smirking at me as he approaches. "Aren't you a good little pet?"

I blush and lower my eyes, at once noticing that he's carrying something with him. In his right hand, he's carrying a canvas tote bag, which he places right in front of me.

"Why so dapper today?" I ask him, shyly reconnecting my gaze with his. "Any special occasion?"

He winks at me. "Who says I'm not wearing this to impress my pet?"

The heat in my cheeks intensifies. "Are you?"

"Maybe," he says. "I have something for you."

He points to the canvas bag that he placed in front of me. "Look inside."

I nod and follow his command, curious to see what he has brought me. He has brought me things before, usually little packages that were wrapped up so beautifully that I felt bad for ripping them open. But those packages have always been smaller than this bag, and they usually contained lingerie or jewelry he wanted me to wear for him. Is this a special new outfit he ordered for me?

I begin rummaging through the bag, not sure if I can trust my eyes when I realize what it is.

"Beautiful clothes," I say, my voice filled with wonder as I look back up at him. "For me?"

He chuckles. "Of course."

I'm so startled, I don't know what to say. For almost two weeks now, he has been insisting that I remain naked, or almost naked, for him at all times. He has repeatedly told me that I won't be wearing any clothes for a while, and that I should never ask for anything, but instead comply with his wish to see as much of my naked body on display as possible every time he walks in.

Does this mean he's letting me go?

The bag contains two outfits, a casual option with a light beige shirt with a deep waterfall neckline, a matching cardigan, and dark blue skinny jeans, and the other is a slinky cocktail dress in a very similar color to the red fur coat.

"For... when?" I ask him, unsure what to make of this. "And... where?"

"For whenever I allow you to wear it, or tell you to," he says.

I wrinkle my eyebrows. Why can he never give me a precise answer to my questions? He must know this is all so confusing to me.

Unless this is part of that deal I should know about. The deal he made with the *real* Ruby Red. Is this another one of those times when he expects me to just understand because it was in the contract I supposedly signed?

"Thank you," I say, knowing that it's expected of me.

"I want you to wear something for me right now," he says, gesturing toward the clothes in my lap. "The casual outfit. I want to see what your ass looks like in those tight jeans."

I nod and get up to get dressed. It's weird how quickly one can get accustomed to not wearing clothes. The upscale fabric of the shirt feels weird against my skin when I slip it on, so strange and unfamiliar. The strange sensation is even stronger with the jeans.

I'm surprised to find that everything fits perfectly. Then again, he has studied my body enough over the past few days to get a good idea of what size I might be.

He looks pleased when I present myself to him, the first time I've been fully dressed since he took me.

"Very good," he comments. "Just one thing, though."

He steps closer and his hands reach up to my throat, unfastening the collar that has been around my neck constantly for the past eleven days. I'm dumbfounded by his action, and equally surprised to find myself somewhat disappointed. It almost makes me feel... naked.

"Are you letting me go?" I ask, my heart heavy with fear. Now that I'm confronted with this possibility, I cannot bear the thought of leaving this house. Of leaving *him*. How am I supposed to just go back to my old life after all of this? How am I supposed to go on with a life that now seems to have so little to offer?

My thoughts scare me, but I cannot help it. I don't want to leave. I want to stay here, with him, following our twisted routine. This is my new constant. I don't know how to go on without him, out there, by myself.

But he's shaking his head. I'm almost relieved.

"Of course not," he says, as if it should be obvious to me. "It's time for a change."

I don't know what he's implying with that comment, but he doesn't give me time to ask.

"For now, I want you to come with me," he says. "And have breakfast with me."

He takes my hand, not leading me by the collar for the first time. We approach the door of my room, the door that leads to the corridor.

"Breakfast?" I ask, bewildered. "You mean... downstairs?"

He lets out a little chuckle as he turns around to face me.

"Yes, downstairs," he answers, and then he opens the door for me.

CHAPTER 32

JOSEPH

She shouldn't be here. Every part of me knows that she shouldn't be here. I'm breaking the rules in a way that's ten times worse than anything she has ever done.

But I cannot help myself.

With these girls, I've always done whatever came to me. I've always followed whatever intrinsic wish I felt like, not holding myself to any rules, only them. The rules exist because I know what I want and what I don't want at any given time.

So, in a way, I'm still following that rule. I'm doing something *I* want to do, something that feels right to do with her. As Ruby walks quietly next to me, so pretty, I'm surprised to find myself wanting *exactly* this. I want to see her in casual clothes, and I want to do casual, everyday things with her.

It's nothing to be afraid of. In a way, it can be expected after all this time. I've never done this, I've never had the girlfriend experience. It's new to me, exotic almost. Trying out new things has always filled me with the thrill I need, the thrill I need to maintain balance.

So what if my newest adventure is being normal, normal like an ordinary person?

She's tense as she walks next to me, her eyes wandering at everything around her as we make our way down the stairs. It's hard to tell whether she's just looking around out of curiousity, or if she's looking for ways to get away. She knows she shouldn't even try anything of that sort because it would make our contract null and void. Everything she has done so far would be mean nothing, she wouldn't receive her compensation, and she wouldn't get far legally either, if that was her aim.

But she's still playing her part to perfection. As real as her terror was in the beginning, I can't risk that she may be thinking about trying to escape.

When we reach the first floor and I lead her to the kitchen and dining area, her gaze turns to plain amazement as she takes in the high-ceilinged room. Bright sunlight is shafting through the wide french doors and floor-length windows, bathing the area in its warm light, while the frost-covered grass outside is a clear indication of the crisp temperatures. The amount of light filtering through the windows coats the entire kitchen in an ethereal glow.

"Wow," she breathes. "This is beautiful!"

She's right. This room has always been my grandmother's favorite place, and I can see why. The French-style kitchen is decorated in mostly ivory colors, with only the counter tops making a stark contrast with their dark gray granite finish.

I cannot remember the last time I had someone else down here. I don't entertain in this house, unless it's for a business meeting, and those are usually held in the reception hall. The only other person who's down here on a regular basis is my main maid Marjory. But she has only been here once since I took Ruby in, and that was just to quickly clean the lower floors, something she hurried to do while I paced up and down the halls, nervous about having one of my staff here while I have a slave upstairs. Marjory knows about the situation, at least partially, and she's only allowed entry to the house because I can count on her discretion.

It still makes me nervous to know that she's coming by today while I'm out of the house. It's simply a matter of bad timing because I promised her that she could have a week off after this so she can go see her newest grandson, and at that point, I didn't know I would have this meeting in town today, of all days.

It'll be okay. Why wouldn't it be? Even if Ruby notices someone else is in the house, why would she cause any trouble? I convince myself that it will all be okay and that she won't scream like hell if she thinks the maid will help her escape.

"Sit," I tell her, pointing toward the dining table that's already laid out for us. "And stay seated."

She casts me a cautious look before she obliges and sits in one of the chairs.

"Can I help you somehow?" she asks when she sees me rummaging through the kitchen, but I tell her no.

"You just sit, and I'll be there in a minute."

I prepare the same food she's been eating for breakfast since she arrived. Incidentally, it's my favorite breakfast, a very rich and hearty meal, perfect for after an exhausting workout. I usually get my workout out of the way in the morning and hardly ever miss a day. I need it to stay fit, and installing a home gym was one of the first things I did when I moved in here.

I place the usual portion of bacon, eggs, toast, and avocado in front of her, as well as a carafe of steaming coffee.

She's visibly confused by this and looks at me as if I have lost my mind. Maybe I have.

"Let me at least pour the coffee," she says, just as I'm about to reach for the carafe.

I have to laugh at her eagerness to serve me. I may be able to train her more thoroughly than I originally thought.

"Go ahead," I tell her, beckoning for her to pour our coffees.

She casts me a grateful smile, and I watch as she serves the savory brew.

"So is that your new thing now?" she asks, changing to a sassy tone I haven't heard from her before. "Are we pretending to be a couple now?"

Her question angers and amuses me at the same time. It shouldn't surprise me that this puzzles her, but I don't like her making fun of me.

"Don't get cocky with me," I say, casting her a warning look. "I told you, good girls get a treat."

"And have I been a good girl?" she asks, before taking a bite of her toast.

"Very much so," I reply without looking at her. She doesn't need to know every detail about what's going on inside my head. Hell, I don't even understand it myself. When I came into her room this morning, I had no intention of following her into the shower. I had no intention of making her mine like this, by fucking her bare against the wet tiles, being consumed by the most amazing orgasm I've had in a while, maybe ever.

Just thinking about it brings my cock back to life. I'm getting hard just looking at her, even now. I just emptied my balls inside her, but I don't think I can leave the house without fucking her again.

"Do good girls also get to ask questions?" she wants to know.

"That depends," I say. "What kind of questions?"

She shrugs.

"Just random things," she says. "Like we're having a conversation."

"Alright," I say, sensing danger. "But I can't promise answers."

She smiles at me, and I hate the effect it has on me.

"What's your name?" she wants to know. "That one should be easy to answer."

I furrow my eyebrows at her. Telling her my name would be another breach of our contract. She knows that I chose to remain anonymous and that there's no reason for us to exchange names. She's to call me Master and I will call her Pet. We don't need any names besides those.

It's bad enough that I called her by her agency name a few days ago. It was a dumb slip-up, a mistake made in the heat of the moment. But I'm in my right mind now, calm and collected, and not in the mood to add further confusion to the situation.

"You know I can't tell you that," I tell her. "And I won't."

CHAPTER 33

LIANA

S o, he can't tell me his name?
You know that.

Again, he's implying that I know something that I actually don't. It's satisfying to realize that I must be right about my assumption, but it also scares me.

I scare myself. I'm not using this information like a sane person should, but instead I've started to dig a hole for myself. Isn't there a chance that he will find out about his mistake? And what about the other woman? What about the real Ruby Red? If she still expecting to be 'kidnapped' by him? And at what point, when it doesn't happen, will she contact him? Shouldn't there be a woman out there who's just as confused as I am? As confused as I am about being here, this other woman must be just as confused about *not* being here.

"I know you can't tell me," I lie to him. "But I thought we could make an exception."

He shakes his head, his facial expression hardening. "We can't."

"You're stubborn," I tell him, watching him with intent to make sure I'm not going too far.

"No," he objects, averting my eyes and focusing on the food in front of him. "I'm not stubborn, just strict. Flexibility is not really my thing when it comes to rules. Another thing you should know."

"You made an exception with this," I say, gesturing toward the food. "And with giving me clothes. Didn't you say those things weren't part of the game either?"

"Game?" he asks, sneering at me. "Stop calling it that."

I bite my lower lip. Okay, that one went too far. I have to be more careful, if I don't want him to cut the conversation short again.

"So, um, are you living here by yourself?" I ask, trying to sound as nonchalant as possible, which only makes my question sound even more stupid.

He furrows his eyebrows at me again.

"Well, not at the moment," he says. "You're here, too."

I roll my eyes at him, something that would usually make him furious, but this time it causes him to laugh. This must be the first time I've ever seen him laugh out loud like this. There's never been more than a quick chuckle or a smirk before.

I smile at him, which causes his face to harden.

"So, it's just you otherwise?" I press, unwilling to let go of my line of questioning.

He nods. "Yes, it's just me."

"Isn't it weird to live in such a big house all by yourself?" I ask. "Doesn't it get lonely?"

"A lot of people live by themselves," he says. "That doesn't mean they are lonely."

I nod. "Yes, sure, but—"

"Do you live by yourself?" he interrupts me.

I bring the coffee mug up to my face, taking a big sip, as if I was trying to hide behind it. My first instinct is to deny it and tell him that I'm living with my boyfriend. It's not even because I *want* to lie to him, but because that's what still pops into my head when I'm asked about my living situation. Luke and I haven't been living together for that long, but it felt so natural to me that I still can't believe it's over.

"Yes, I do," I say. "As of late."

"And are you lonely?" he wants to know.

I pause, placing the mug back on the table, absent-mindedly turning it on the small bottom plate. The sun rays are playing on the cutlery, randomly blinding me with sharp flashes of light as he moves his fork and knife before me.

"Yes," I whisper solemnly without looking at him. "Yes, I am lonely."

I can feel his eyes on me, but I don't reciprocate the gaze. I don't even know why I'm telling him this. He doesn't want to hear my little sob story. He just wants to have fun with his little sex slave and not be burdened with her emotional luggage.

He doesn't say a word, but reaches for his own coffee mug, taking his sweet time sipping from it. This is awkward for him, and he doesn't know how to react.

"This was my grandparents' house," he says after a few more moments of uncomfortable silence have passed between us. "I used to live here with them, partly grew up here. It feels more like home to me than any other place."

He pauses, waiting for me to lift my chin to look at him. Our eyes meet across the table, our gazes speaking silently to one another. His face speaks of concern and empathy. Even if he's only faking it to make me feel better, he's doing a really good job at it.

"Maybe that's why I don't feel lonely," he adds, his words heavy with meaning. "Despite the vast and empty halls. Every room echoes voices from the past. It's hard to feel alone among them."

I'm struck by how beautiful his words are, just like the man who spoke them. It's hard to imagine that this is the same man who enslaved me, the same man who locked me up, who whips and spanks me, and who fucks me like a savage.

"Your grandparents?" I ask. "You lived here with your grandparents?"

He nods. "Yes, they moved to Florida and gave this house to me."

"What about your parents?" I want to know.

His face changes, and now he's the one who's avoiding my eyes.

"They're gone," he says. "Not much to say about them."

"I'm sorry, I—"

"Don't worry, it happened a long time ago. I was still a kid," he says. "It doesn't bother me."

He takes a big bite of his toast and looks at me squarely, burying any hint of sadness that might have been there a second before.

"What about your parents?" he asks.

I'm confused at his question. He has never asked me anything personal, and I didn't expect him to, especially after I found out that he thinks I'm just a whore he bought for his pleasure.

"They're alive," I reply. "I think."

He chuckles. "You think?"

"Well, the sperm donor who's supposed to be my father did nothing but drink and hit me and my mother until she finally had the guts to kick him out when I was nine," I tell him. "And my mother married another asshole shortly after that and had another kid with him. He's not as bad as my father used to be, but he hates me and I hate him. They are still up in Maine, we barely talk."

"So you're not from here?"

I shake my head. "No, I moved here for a job."

He turns to me, drawing in his eyebrows as his casts me a skeptical look.

Damn, that was stupid. Who would move to a different state just to become a whore?

"Er, not *this* job," I correct myself. "I mean, it—"

"I don't need to know," he interrupts me. "But I'm sorry to hear about your family."

Now he's the one trying to console me just like I did for him before.

We continue to eat in silence for a few moments. There's so much more I want to know about him. There was such a deep sadness behind his words when he talked about this house and how its halls are filled with voices from the past. I wonder if those voices also echo fights and yelling, as they would in my family's home.

"How did your parents die?" I dare to ask, certain that he will deny me a response.

"Car accident," he says. "My father was wasted and drove their car into a ravine. Killed them both, but luckily no one else was hurt. I was with my grandparents at the time."

"Fuck," I gasp, unable to come up with a better remark.

"Amen to that," he says. "Guess we both have that in common, fucked-up fathers."

He casts me a weird look, questioning, searching, as if he was trying to find something else hidden behind my exterior.

"I guess so," I say, raising my coffee mug to him in a toast.

CHAPTER 34

JOSEPH

I check the time once we're done eating our food, and I'm relieved to see that I still have a few minutes before I have to get on my way to Boston.

Time has flown by while we were sitting here eating together. We have been downstairs for more than an hour, but it didn't feel like any time had passed at all. Talking to her comes so easily to me, it feels natural, right. I shouldn't be surprised to learn what I did about her family's past. No girl ends up as an escort if she grew up in a healthy family environment. There's always something wrong with them, and just like in her case, it's most often the father to blame.

I guess the same could be said about me, but I refrain from blaming my father for anything that I've done or who I've become. He doesn't deserve the attention.

He hasn't even earned the right to be blamed for my misdeeds.

I pour us another coffee, not ready to return Ruby to her room upstairs. This will be an exception. I won't bring her downstairs again because it would be a stupid thing for me to do. But since it's just this one time, I might as well make the most of it.

She's holding on to her coffee mug, looking so innocent, almost too prim and proper in the outfit I gave her to wear, and it's hard to believe she's a prostitute. She strikes me as too smart and timid for that profession. I wonder what was really behind it.

Maybe she's in trouble? A good girl who made a bad decision, or somehow got caught up in some kind of shady business and now owes a bunch of money to some bad people, perhaps?

Or maybe she simply enjoys it, though knowing her as I do, I can't believe that.

I would love to ask her, but that would be such a big breach. We can talk about our families, but not about her real job, and definitely not about the reason why she's here.

"There's something else I'm curious about," she says, casting me a cautious look.

"I'm not surprised to hear that," I say, leaning back in my chair, as I beckon her to continue speaking. "What is it?"

"Your tattoos," she says. "They are quite... peculiar."

I smile to myself. "That's an interesting word for it."

"What do they mean?" she adds. "I mean, why did you get those particular ones?"

I hesitate, looking at her as I contemplate my answer. The truth may scare her, and it would tell her a lot more about me, and I'm not sure that I want to share. I'd rather say nothing than to lie to her.

"They remind me of something," I say, deliberately being vague in my answer. "Or rather of some*one*."

"Your father?" she guesses.

I snort.

"Fuck no," I say. "He doesn't deserve to be remembered."

"Well, who then?" Ruby presses, leaning forward with interest.

"Myself," I tell her. "They remind me of the person I used to be but no longer want to be."

Her eyes flicker with anxious fascination. "What kind of person?"

"An angry person, very angry," I reply. "I was an angry child, and I wasn't very good at handling my emotions. I let it out on other people."

"So you beat up other kids?"

"Yes, a lot," I confirm. "I constantly was getting into trouble, and I wasn't shy about using my fists. I've always been tall and strong, and I used it to my advantage. I did some real damage."

That's the understatement of the year, but she doesn't need to hear the entire truth. She doesn't need to know that I almost killed another boy when I was sixteen. She doesn't need to know that I robbed him of his ability to walk for the rest of his life, and she doesn't need to know that I took out an eye from another kid shortly before that. Those two were only the tip of the iceberg, but they were also the last ones.

I will never get those images out of my head, no matter how hard I try. They will haunt me forever. The boy, lying on the floor before me in a puddle of his own blood, motionless, so badly ravaged that I wasn't the only one who thought he was dead. He survived, his life was changed forever, while I continue to walk the Earth being able to use both of my legs. No amount of money that my family paid out to him will ever make up for the fact that he will never walk again. *He* can't forget about that day, and when I—with the help of my grandfather—decided to make a change in my life, I wanted to make sure that I could never forget about it either.

The marks on my skin resemble the scars left on my victims. They aren't pretty, and they don't look anything like the kinds of tattoo men usually get, but they serve a purpose. They aren't designed to be vain decorations, but rather to help me never to forget.

"So you really hurt people?" she asks, her voice tight and concerned.

I nod. "Yes, I really hurt people."

Ruby's eyes are locked on me, observing me. I can see her mind working, processing what I just explained. She doesn't look scared, but only because she's working so hard at hiding it.

"I don't anymore," I tell her. "And I would never hurt you."

She takes a deep breath, relaxing her shoulders a little.

"I want to believe that," she says, sounding anything but convinced.

Seeing her like this drives me insane. That real and raw fear pervading her entire being. She's too good of an actress—or too tricked into thinking that all of this is real. I don't want her to feel this way, not like this. It fucking bothers me.

"You can trust me on that," I tell her, reaching for her hand on the table. She doesn't flinch, but welcomes my touch as a reassurance, intertwining her fingers with mine as she smiles at me.

"I have no choice, do I?" she says.

The smile on her face is lined with sadness. I wish she wouldn't look at me like that.

"Will you let me clear the table?" she asks, nodding toward the dishes in front of us.

I raise an eyebrow at her. "Why?"

"I would like to," she says, shrugging. "I haven't done anything since I... got here. I'd like to be useful."

"You *are* useful to me," I tell her. "Very much so."

The blush that rises on her cheeks is so much more appealing than her frightened sorrow from before.

"Alright, if it makes you happy, clear the table," I say.

Ruby smiles as she gets up from her seat, gathering our plates and carrying them over to the kitchen as my eyes follow her. She knows that I'm watching her, and she makes sure to move her hips in a way that emphasizes her round ass in those tight jeans I bought for her. I knew she'd look delicious in them.

She deliberately bends over, taunting me by poking her ass out as she places the dishes on the counter top. The effect it has on me is clearly visible in my crotch. I rub across the hardness between my legs, checking my watch one more time.

"You said you wanted to be useful," I say, as I get up from my chair to follow her to where she's standing in the kitchen.

She turns around to face me, a mischievous smirk brightening her pretty face when she sees me unbuckling my belt.

CHAPTER 35

LIANA

He left. This is the first time he's left the house since I've been here, at least as far as I know. He could have left at times when I was taking a nap. I have so little to do, and I am often so exhausted from the things we do together that midday naps have become a habit.

Today is different. I was still stirred up from our shower session when he took me downstairs to have breakfast with him. He may think that I was trying to be a good girl for him, but when he fucked me on the kitchen counter, it really was all about me. I took what I needed from him, savoring it as he rammed his considerable length inside me, climaxing in record time.

He looked confused when I thanked him afterward, but equally pleased. He never mentioned anything about leaving, but now that I see a car driving away, I'm all the more happy about that kitchen quickie. I so desperately needed it, and I hate the longing sadness that overcomes me as I realize I'm alone.

The windows in my room are facing in such a way that it tells me very little about this house and its location. I cannot see the entrance or the driveway from here, but I can guess that it must be to the left, around the corner.

I wonder why he didn't tell me that he was leaving. Does he not want me to realize that I'm here by myself?

After he fucked me in the kitchen, he urged me to go back to my room immediately, not even letting me finish up clearing the table.

"It will be dealt with," he said when I asked about it, and I figured that he meant that he would take care of it. But he left just a few moments after locking the door to my room, visibly in a hurry.

I'm standing at the window, looking out across the vast landscape surrounding the mansion. I wonder if he'd tell me where we are if I ask. It's very unlikely, and I have a feeling that this is just another part of the deal, not knowing where we are. If this is all a paid and planned set-up, I'm pretty sure there's also a time frame attached to it. A time frame I'm supposed to know about, so I can't ask him about *that* either.

A part of me wishes I really was the woman he ordered, or at least that I knew what she knows about this. She probably knows a lot more about him, too. His name, his age, his occupation, mundane stuff like that.

Not knowing bothers me. I may have figured out bits and pieces, but I still have so many questions. And even worse, I feel myself getting attached to this man, and I'm sure that's definitely not part of the deal.

It's just a twist of fate that I'm here under his control instead of the woman he originally thought he was getting. Me of all people. In my mind, I've been traveling to dark places like what this whole experience has been like, many times before. I've touched myself to the fantasies buzzing in my brain of being bound and forced to obey. I've begged Luke to spank and choke me when we were together, but he was appalled by me, and he told me I was broken and sick.

I always knew I wasn't normal, and I knew I wasn't attracted to normal. I stayed with Luke because I hoped those dark desires would go away. If you act normal long enough, it must become part of the routine, right?

Now since this man took me, it has reversed all my efforts to become normal, peeling away layer after layer to reveal the warped mind underneath. And I'm beginning to love every moment of it. I don't want to lose it. I want to know how much further we can go together, how deep this can get.

My hand wanders up to my empty throat, tracing along the lines where the collar used to be. He never put it back on after bringing me back upstairs. I wonder if this morning was the beginning of our goodbye? Is he preparing me for my departure?

Just as I want to turn away from the window and retreat to the bed for another nap, something catches my attention. It's a car arriving at the house. I barely ever see cars on the country road passing by the house, and if I do, they're usually just driving by.

My first hope is that he's returning, but I realize it's not his car. This one is red and doesn't look nearly as expensive as the one he was driving. And it's slowing down in front of the house, disappearing from my view.

I hurry over to the door to my room, closing my eyes and pressing my ear against the crack of the doorframe to listen for possible movement downstairs.

My eyes open wide when I actually hear the sound of a heavy door opening and closing. It must be the front door. I hold my breath when I can hear footsteps moving around on the first floor. They sound different than the steps I hear when he's moving around in the house. These are faster and smaller, and they are loud on the tiled floor in the entrance area. Heels. It must be a woman.

I take a deep breath, focusing on the sound as the steps fade away. I'm not familiar enough with the floor plan of the house to know where the person might be heading, but I can tell that she isn't coming upstairs.

This could be it. My first chance to speak to another person since arriving here. My chance to get all the answers I'm seeking.

My chance to get away.

And yet, I don't make a sound. I don't scream for help. I don't bang against the door. I just sit there, on my floor, in the room that has become my prison for the past two weeks.

Quietly waiting until I hear the front door open and close again, watching from the window as the red car drives away from the house. Leaving me here alone again.

CHAPTER 36

JOSEPH

I should have known that I'm not good at making exceptions. Exceptions tend to become the rule in my case. They don't call it a slippery slope for nothing.

It's day thirteen, two days since I removed her training collar and brought her downstairs with me to have breakfast together like a freaking married couple.

And now I'm doing it again. I'm making a fuss about something that is heavy with meaning, as if this was a true relationship, but should be nothing more in our case than a simple transition.

Tonight, she will receive a new collar, a permanent one that she won't be able to take off. Not until our time together comes to an end. The fact that there is a definite end to our arrangement is the difference. I hate thinking about it.

She earned her collar, unlike many others before her. It's my way of showing her that she's truly special to me, even if the gesture goes beyond her understanding.

I know she misses it, she's been asking about it, mentioning that her neck feels 'weirdly bare' now that I took it off. She cast me questioning looks all day yesterday, probably wondering if she gave me any reason to be unsatisfied with her. Taking the collar feels like a punishment to her, which shows that she's ready for the next step.

But I don't know if she fully understands the meaning behind a more permanent collar, or if she'll feel the same way once she realizes she won't be able to take it off.

She has received clear instructions, and I can rely on her newfound willingness to obey. I told her to put on the slinky red dress and doll herself up a little. This time, she will wear a sexy pair of stockings under her dress, and this time she'll beg me to fuck her once we're done with everything else.

She'll be my queen tonight, until it's time to treat her otherwise.

While I do cook on a regular basis, in no way am I capable of creating something special enough for the occasion, so I make another exception and ask my personal chef to stop by in the afternoon to prepare a meal for us. Something light yet elaborate, the exact opposite of my style of cooking.

I'm wearing the same suit I wore two days ago, knowing that she'll appreciate it. The way she looked at me suggested that she liked it a lot, and it was confirmed when she invited me to fuck her for a second time that morning. She's turning into such a perfect little pet that I'm already dreading the day when I'll have to let her go.

She's kneeling in the middle of the room, wearing the red dress that hugs her slim frame so tightly that she's forced to keep her legs closed in a modest way. Her chin lifts when she hears me approaching, but her eyes don't open until I kiss her, silently giving her permission to look at me.

"You look beautiful," I praise her. "Wait here."

She's well-behaved enough to not turn her head when I walk over to the connected room to fetch something else from the cabinet that she'll wear during our dinner.

"Get up," I order her once I step back inside her room, watching as she gets up on her feet. She's wearing the heels I took from her on the first day because I knew they would look good with the dress. Her hair is styled in a pinned up-do, another thing I asked her to do.

"You've been complaining about your neck being so bare these past two days," I begin, while I circle around her, taking in her breathtaking view before I come to a halt in front of her.

She's smiling at me, beaming with joyful anticipation.

"Am I getting it back?" she asks.

I shake my head, not missing the hint of disappointment on her face.

"No," I tell her. "You're getting something nicer."

Her face lights up when I reach inside the pocket of my suit jacket, producing a new collar for her to wear. It's a black leather collar, just like the one she had before, but this one has a heart-shaped lock at the front instead of a simple d-ring.

"The first one was just a training collar," I tell her. "This one is different. This says you're mine. You won't be able to take it off on your own."

"I never took off the other one either," she says, her eyes casting back and forth between me and the collar in my hand.

"Yes, that's why you deserve this one," I continue. "You've been a very good girl for me. I'm a pleased Master, ready to collar my pet."

Her breathing changes when I step forward to lock the collar around her neck. She's panting with excitement, her gray-blue eyes sparkling with anticipation as my hands caress the sensitive skin around her neck.

A sigh escapes her lush lips when the lock clicks shut. I don't need a key to close it, just to open it, and if everything goes according to plan, I won't open this lock before another twenty-six days have passed. That's when the contract ends and I will have to let her go, something I need to keep reminding myself of because it seems too hard to believe.

"Thank you," she breathes, radiating a happiness that is so raw and honest, that I truly want to believe its sincerity.

"Thank you for being such a good pet," I tell her. "Earning your submission is a pleasure."

With her, it really feels like I had to earn it, despite the knowledge that she's going to be paid handsomely for this. She made me fight for it, she made me do things I'd normally never even consider. She deserves so much more than this.

"We're having dinner downstairs tonight to mark the special occasion," I let her know. "But before we go, there's something else I want you to wear."

She nods without knowing what I might be referring to, and I'm sure she's expecting some kind of jewelry.

Well, she's not entirely wrong about that. I reach into my other pocket, revealing a little diamond plug. She looks at with bewildered fascination and curiosity.

"Is that...?"

I step closer, placing my index finger on her lips to stop her from speaking, replacing it with my lips a moment later. She moans when I claim her with a kiss, responding to me like she should, her body squirming against mine with need. I reach around, tracing along the small of her back, before traveling beneath her sexy dress. She was asked to wear nothing but stockings underneath, and she obeyed her orders. I don't even have to tell her to spread her legs for me. She does it all on her own, greedily leaning into my touch, as I part her lips to fondle the wetness between them.

"Fuck, Ruby," I breathe between our kisses. "So wet for me, what a good pet you are."

She smiles, moaning as I trace the tip of the plug along her wet lips, gently pushing the tip inside her, before retreating, gathering up more of her juices as I allow my fingers to trail along her core. This is not meant for her pussy.

She gasps when I grab her ass with the other hand, spreading her cheeks apart while teasing her tight hole with the dampened tip of the plug.

"That's right," I breathe. "This will spread your tight little ass for me."

She sighs heartily when I force the plug inside, smoothly pushing until it sits securely. I tap on it a few times, testing her reaction to it. Ruby is panting in my arms, while she accommodates the feeling of the plug stretching her. Her dainty hands crawl into the fabric of my suit, pulling us even closer together.

"Do you like it?" I whisper in her ear.

"Yes," she replies breathlessly. "Yes, Master."

CHAPTER 37

LIANA

This is both the most agonizing and most wonderful dinner I've ever had in my life. We're sitting opposite one another and dining on a spread of light tapas, each dish so exquisite that I relish every single bite. Cured olives, lucques, an assortment of steamed vegetables each with its own surprisingly characteristic taste, and a small selection of undoubtedly expensive cheeses, topped off with a bottle of exquisite red wine that tastes divine and probably costs more than my apartment's monthly rent.

I've never been wined and dined like this, never been treated to such a lavish dinner, and definitely never while wearing a diamond anal plug. It's such an intriguing sensation that I can't calm down. I'm so pleasantly agitated that it's a struggle for me to concentrate on the food and wine.

"You look tense," he teases me, as he has often does.

I reach for my crystal wine glass, casting him a sassy smile as I take another sip.

"I'm fine," I say. "Thank you for this wonderful dinner."

"I'm glad you're enjoying it," he says. "You like getting your ass spread, too, don't you?"

The suddenness with which he poses an unexpected question like this gets me every time.

"I do," I say, blushing and shying away from his gaze.

"Describe how it feels to me," he says.

I ignore his command, instead keeping myself occupied with another bite of the steamed and spiced vegetables. I never knew that a simple piece of cauliflower could taste this good.

"Pet," he admonishes. "Describe it to me."

My eyes meet his, my heart jumping under his warning gaze. His deep-searching demeanor reaches a part of me that has never been touched before, and I can't help but respond to it in the way I do.

"I'm not good at describing things," I tell him, afraid of embarrassing myself.

"You'll have to learn how then," he says. "Go ahead, describe the feeling to me."

Oh, for God's sake. Why this? I've never been a fan of dirty talk, mainly because I suck at it and feel like an idiot every time I try. It's so much easier for me to follow other commands, like getting on my knees, posing for him, sucking on his exquisitely exciting cock.

"I'm more of a doer than a talker," I reply, winking at him across the table.

I was hoping this remark would steer him in another direction, to one I'm more comfortable with, maybe asking me to show him something or do something instead of making me say things.

But he's doesn't move on.

"Describe it to me," he repeats, emphasizing every syllable.

I roll my eyes at him, something I know he hates. It works like a charm if I want to get his attention in a certain way.

"Did you just roll your eyes at me?" he wants to know, leaning back in his chair with his hand resting on the table, impatiently tapping with his fingers.

"Maybe," I reply in an intentionally sassy tone.

"You know what I think of that," he says. "I give you a collar, wine and dine you like a perfect gentleman, and you roll your eyes at me when I ask you to do one simple thing?"

I smirk at him. His tone is changing, and so is the expression on his face. The candlelight is dancing in his hazel eyes, giving life to a spark that exists there.

"It's not a simple thing," I say. "It's silly. I don't like talking about it."

I've never teased him like this, and I love the way his expression changes from moment to moment, waiting for me to retreat, trying to follow his order because I'm too scared of the consequences.

But I'm not scared. Not tonight.

I'm both horny and curious to see what he will do if I keep going on like this. I know this is not serious enough of an offense for me to end up in the attic, but it will hurt. It's been too long since I've felt those harshly placed and deliberate stings on my skin. I crave them more than I knew possible.

"Watch it, my pet," he warns one more time. "You're walking on thin ice."

I hesitate for a moment, trying to come up with something else I could do to get what I want. But I've never been a very creative person.

"Uh oh, thin ice," I mock, rolling my eyes again. "What, oh, what, could that mean?"

I wince when he jumps up from his chair. A mixture of delicious fear and lust shoots through my body when he circles the table to approach me, grabbing my upper arm and pulling me up on my feet.

He pulls me close, wrapping his arms around my body, one hand traveling under my dress. He applies pressure on the toy inserted in my ass, causing me to gasp. His face is so close to mine that we're almost kissing.

"So that's how you want to play tonight?" he asks in a hoarse whisper. "You want a real inauguration?"

My eyes are locked on his, reciprocating the fierceness with which he looks at me.

"I want pain," I tell him. "Show me how far it can go."

His eyes flicker with understanding, a dark warning fleeting through them that makes my heart jump.

I yelp out in surprise when he lifts me up as if I weigh nothing, turning around and marching out of the kitchen while carrying me over his shoulder like prey.

"Let's hope you don't regret this."

LIANA

I know that things will be serious this time when he brings me up to the dark play room next to my bedroom.

He turns to me, scanning me from head to toe.

"That dress looks lovely on you," he says, and just when I want to thank him for the compliment, he steps forward and pulls it down off my shoulder and draws down the zipper in one swift motion. The dress falls down to puddle around my feet, leaving me almost naked. I'm wearing nothing but the stockings and a black garter belt underneath, and he stares at me hungrily with his approving gaze.

"This looks even better," he says, stepping forward to pull me in for a kiss. I know he can't resist the desire to touch me when I'm standing this exposed in front of him. I'm not surprised to feel his hand slip between my legs, urging me to spread them apart. I moan through our kiss when he slides his thick fingers along my damp entrance, humming with approval as he's met with my dripping warm juices.

"So excited already," he breathes after he breaks our kiss. "Get on there."

He gestures toward the black leather bench that looks like a pommel horse. "Knees here, wrists over there."

I follow his instructions and place myself on the horse as requested. He repositions me a little, so that my core is exposed on the edge, while I support myself on my knees and wrists. He fastens the shackles around my wrists first, making sure that they fit securely, but not too tight by wiggling them, and then he does the same around my knees.

"What do you think will happen now?" he asks. He's now standing at my back, his eyes resting on me as he watches me adjust to the bench.

"A spanking?" I ask, hope radiating in my voice.

He chuckles and walks over to the cabinet. My eyes follow him, as he opens the glass door.

"You say that as if you're looking forward to it," he says. "Remember, this is a punishment."

"I *am* looking forward to it," I tell him.

He doesn't go for a whip or a flogger this time, both utensils I'm familiar with. I know what the pain of leather strings cutting into the flesh on your behind feels like. But I don't know how it feels to be hit with a paddle, which is what he takes from the cabinet. It's about as large as both of his hands put together and made of wood.

He sees my eyes widening in anxious fascination, as he walks back to the bench, approaching me with a dark promise in his smile.

"Read this for me," he says as he holds the paddle up to my face.

A smile plays around the corners of my mouth when I see what's written on the wooden paddle in mirrored text.

"Pet," I read out loud.

"Good girl," he praises me, tracing the paddle along my spine as he moves to the back of the bench.

"It's time for you to learn your place," he says, gently caressing my left ass cheek with the paddle as he speaks. "This will be written all over your perfect ass when I'm done with you. Would you like that?"

"Yes, Master," I breathe, shivering with anticipation when he lifts the paddle up, only to move it over to my right side and stroke it along the curve of my other cheek.

"But you know what?" he says. "It's not going to be easy to leave an imprint. It'll take a while—and a lot of force. It will hurt, my pet. But that's what you asked for, right?"

I close my eyes in shame. Admitting to my wishes is still the hardest part of all of this.

"Yes, Master," I utter.

He lifts the paddle again, and I tense up to prepare myself for the first strike. But it doesn't come. For moments that seem to stretch into eternity, he just lets me wait, trembling with expectation, my breathing accelerating with each passing second.

When the first blow finally does come, it doesn't feel nearly as bad as I anticipated. He hits my left cheek, then my right, both with strong, but endurable slaps.

"That's not going to leave a mark, Master," I cautiously remark.

I hear him huff behind me.

"Impatient, are we?" he says, before unleashing two more beats on my skin. Each of them is stronger than the ones before, the pain now spreading through my behind in a ferocious wave.

He lets the paddle fly down on my ass again and again, each whack gaining in strength. I bite my lip, unwilling to give him the satisfaction of crying out in anguish, until I can no longer withhold them. He delivers each blow, never hitting the same spot twice, thus distributing the pain equally over my tortured ass without ever hitting the jewel plug.

"Do you think that was enough?" he asks eventually, interrupting the violent onslaught to my skin.

Tears of agony are running down my cheeks, but I shake my head. "No, Master. I don't think it was."

I can take more, I *know* it, and I want to prove it to him *and* to myself.

"Good girl," he says. "Let me make sure you'll remember who you belong to."

The next impact robs me of my breath, even forbidding me to utter a shriek of pain. The pain is so intense that it blinds me for a split second, leaving me overwhelmed almost to unconsciousness by a feverish vertigo.

He investigates the spot he just hit for a moment, deciding that it was not enough, and this time he hits the exact same spot. The pain is mind-numbing, crippling my senses as it consumes my body.

"Beautiful," I hear his voice from afar.

Sweat is running down the small of my back and at the side of my temples, and I'm panting erratically as I process the crippling and burning after-pain.

But he's not done with me.

"That was one," he announces. "But my adorable pet still has room on her other ass cheek, doesn't she?"

He moves the paddle along the sore skin on my unmarked side and repeats the same routine of maneuvers, leaving two heavy blows on the same spot until he's happy with the result.

I'm weeping involuntarily, shaken by violent sobs, and he finally puts the paddle aside.

"You brought this on yourself, my pet," he tells me, as he caresses the burning skin of my behind. "What do you say?"

"Thank you," I breathe, choking up under my tears. "Thank you, Master."

"Good girl," he replies, moving behind me to fetch something else from a drawer that's out of my line of vision. "But don't thank me yet, we're not done."

For a moment, I fear that he might continue spanking me with another tool, but it seems he has other things on his mind. He places something at my entrance, pressing it against my clit before I hear a clicking sound and then erupt in a frenzied convulsion, as I'm hit with the strongest vibrations I've ever felt on my pussy.

"Too much for you?" he asks, over the sound of the vibrator.

I let out a range of unintelligible groans, but manage to nod my head yes.

"Well, too bad, because I'm not going to stop," he says, applying even more pressure on my sensitive nub.

I emit a chorus of agonizing and pleasurable moans, trying to evade the vibrations to no avail, as I'm tightly secured in place. I can hear the ripping of tape when he affixes the vibrator in place with duct tape, making sure that it won't move, before he comes around to my front, meeting my dazed gaze as he leans forward.

"Today, I want you to count something else," he says. "Today, I want you to come as often as you please. And I want you to tell me every time it happens. Do you understand?"

It almost strikes me as funny that I can feel the first waves of an impending climax just as he poses his demand, and I find myself rolling my eyes back into my head when I give him the response he seeks.

"Yes, Master," I utter, just before the first surge of rapture hits me, shaking my muscles uncontrollably as I ride on the waves of pleasure, prolonged by the continuing vibrations forced on my clit.

"One!" I exclaim, unsure if my release is still ongoing or already evolving into a second swell of euphoria.

"Good girl," he praises me, petting my head before he straightens up and unbuckles his belt in front of my face. His impressive erection springs free when he pulls down his pants, and I instinctively open my mouth, so he can drive himself down my throat.

This is not a simple blow job, as I'm robbed of any control. He fucks my mouth with fierce and wild abandon, and all I can do is keep my teeth from hurting him. I choke on his rod, temporarily distracted from the vibrations still pulsating on my center.

"Next, I want you to come on my cock," he announces, and withdraws his length from my mouth, a line of saliva stretching between us as he moves away and repositions himself behind me.

A pained groan escapes me when he stretches me with his girth, while cupping my tortured ass cheeks. With the jewel plug still in place, his cock feels even more massive inside of me. He adds a new level of agitation to my deliriously tormented center with his cock ramming in and out of me in rhythm with the vibrating toy. I've never felt this completely and utterly at somebody's mercy before. I can't move, I can't object, all I can do is ride on the ebbing and flowing waves of pleasure as they hit me again and again, over and over, nonstop.

"Two!" I yelp as another orgasm pummels my body. I erupt in violent tremors as he continues to fuck me deeply and harshly, his pelvis jamming against my bruised ass with every abrasive thrust.

This climax turns into the longest I've ever had. I'm moaning through my euphoric high, when I can feel his fingers venture somewhere else. I groan loudly when he reaches fort he jewel plug, pulling it out while he continues to fuck me. He puts it aside and massages my tight hole, carefully stretching me with his thumb, while he continues to fuck my pussy.

"This is next," he lets me know, his voice drowned out by the noise of the vibrator. "I'm going to stretch your ass today, my pet."

I gasp, instantly tensing up, because I've never done that before. I've never had a cock buried inside my ass, let alone someone of his size. Then again, I asked for pain, didn't I?

I groan in disappointment when he pulls his cock out of my pussy, leaving me empty and in frantic need for more, seeking balance for the toy playing havoc on my overly sensitive clit. Even after coming twice within such a short time, I still don't feel the relaxed satisfaction that usually follows peaking like this.

His tip teases the entrance of my hole, begging the question how on Earth he's supposed to fit in there. I shriek in agony when he forces himself inside, spreading my tight pucker with his massive girth, moving forward inch by painful inch, the burning sensation intensifying as he breaches the tight ring of muscles.

"Relax, my pet," I hear him say. "You're only making this harder on yourself."

And just as he finishes his sentence, I reach the tipping point between pain and pleasure. His invasion no longer hurts as badly as it did in the beginning. Instead, I'm flushed with a new kind of agitation, my skin glowing with heat and my heart racing, as I pant through the process of accommodating his massive size inside my ass.

"That's a good girl," he says behind me, only fueling my arousal with his praise.

He starts fucking me, slowly at first, my ached shrieks accompanying every thrusting motion, before I start egging him on. I squirm beneath him, moving my hips as much as I can, inviting him to move faster, harder, rougher.

"More," I find myself begging. "Harder. Faster."

It's easier to ask for such things when I don't have his face in front of me, but I still feel the heat of embarrassment as I verbalize my wishes.

"What a good, slutty pet," he comments, grabbing me firmly by the hip and driving himself into me with a savage force I would have thought impossible a few moments ago. This feels different than before. It triggers different parts of my body, even shifting the tormenting tease of the vibrations a little as he stretches my insides with his length.

"I'll join you this time," he announces. "I'll fill that tight ass of yours with my cum."

His naughty words send me over the edge.

"Three!" I howl in a long drawn out exclamation as the most violent exaltation floods my body. I can feel him throbbing as he dumps his release deep inside me, keeping his promise from before. His hands crawl into the skin of my ass, adding the sweet spice of pain to my orgasm.

I feel exhausted and over-stimulated when he pulls himself out of me, spreading my cheeks so he can watch his cum dripping out of my center and down the inside of my thigh while I coil under the ongoing vibrations of the toy.

This is so filthy and twisted. He's bathing in pleasure at the sight of me, rubbing his still hard cock as he comes back to stand in front of me. I moan with anguished bliss when he pulls my head back, forcing me to look up to him while he rubs his dick. Somewhere along the way, he got rid of his suit completely, and he's now standing before me with nothing but the dark tattoos covering his sublime body.

"Three for you, one for me," he says, fixating me with his dark gaze. "But you're not done, are you my slutty little pet?"

I shake my head as best I can, trying to swallow the shame of allowing my tongue to stick out as I yearn for his cock.

"I want to watch you come one more time for me," he says. "Come for me, while my cum is dripping out of your perfect ass."

I blush at his words, shifting my hips a little, so the vibrator hits another spot on my sore clit. I feel so used, adrift and defenseless against facing my own cravings, the same cravings I've been forbidden to fulfill for so long.

The way he looks at me now is exactly what I have been wishing for. There's a certain smugness to it, based on the knowledge that he's doing this for himself just as much as he is for me. He's not appalled by who I am; on the contrary, he exposes those parts of me that even I was too afraid to face until now.

I fail to worry about the sound of my groan when I feel another release approaching. He can see it as soon as I feel it, observing my body's reaction and the emotions painted across my face as I give in to my final climax.

"F-f-four," I stutter helplessly, as my vision is blinded by painful pleasure. I pant and groan through the final fervor as my head begins to spin dizzily and I feel lightheaded.

He tightens his grip around my hair, pulling my face up to his while he reaches another climax himself, unloading on my face this time.

This last peak is brutal and short for both of us, robbing me of my strength entirely. My muscles go completely limp as my head falls forward, and the vibrations turn into nothing but pure torment on my sore and swollen nub.

He lets go of my hair and hurries behind me, finally switching off the toy before unfastening the shackles binding my wrists and ankles. I'm too weak to get up by myself, but he doesn't ask me to. He picks me up in his strong arms, breathing heavily himself, as he carries me over to the bedroom and carefully places me on the soft silk sheets before lying down beside me.

We lay in unison, both panting and smiling dreamily at each other. I never thought that any of this could be possible. Up until now, this was nothing but a dream, a dark fantasy that I never would believe could have a chance of coming true. And now it has.

With this man, who robbed me, and makes me feel like a princess. A twisted princess.

He caresses the heated skin on my cheek, shaking his head as if he can't believe it himself. I don't dare speak because I'm afraid of breaking the loving and peaceful silence between us. But then he does it with a revelation that warms my heart even more.

"Joseph," he breathes. "My name is Joseph."

CHAPTER 39

JOSEPH

Twenty-one days. I can feel the end closing in on us, and I've never hated it more than I do this time. I've been falling further down the slippery slope with each day we spend together. She has taken more of me than any other girl has before, and I cannot imagine having to let her go. So soon.

We've passed the middle point of our time together. This is usually the point where a routine sets in that slowly leads to me losing interest in the girl.

With her, though, it's exactly the opposite.

She's pulling me closer, in deeper, even after I thought it couldn't be possible. We've been spending all our meals together for the past week because I enjoy her company, I like acting normal with her. No one has ever evoked that desire within me. At first, I tried to dismiss it as just another kink, something new I wanted to try because it was foreign to me. But by now even *I'm* willing to admit that this might be more. I just don't know how to deal with it.

Nothing is boring with her. While we still tiptoe around the taboo issue of our arrangement, we talk about pretty much everything else. She's told me about her family, where she grew up, where she went to school, who her friends were. At one point, she even mentioned an old boyfriend who betrayed her in so many ways that it made me sick. I stopped her from talking about him any further because I couldn't bear listening to it.

She has learned to ask the right questions, no longer pressing me about things she know she shouldn't. But she managed to get me to talk about myself, my family, and the parts of my past that I was willing to share. I don't think I've ever talked about myself to anyone as much as I have with her. It's frightening and liberating at the same time. I don't feel like I'm giving away too much, but I often found myself crossing my own limits.

I always stopped when things got too real. When I found myself approaching an area so intimately personal that sharing any more information might get me into real trouble. It's easy to talk about the fuck-up my father was, and how he dragged my mother down with him. It's also easy to talk about my grandparents, my grand-father in particular, who saw not only the symptoms of my troubles, but the root cause of it. He saw something in me that no one else saw, and he made sure to nurture that part of me before other parts could kill it. He knew all I needed was a challenge, a purpose, something that was all mine to control, something that provided me with power and success, but also the burden of responsibility.

In me, he saw the heir to the family's business. He saw the person that my father failed to be.

Ruby's eyes were glued to me every time I talked to her about those things. Her interest is so sincere that, for the first time, I understood what people meant when they said someone "touched their heart". She certainly has that effect on me.

This morning is not the first time for me to wake up next to her. Another rule I broke. I've spent the night with her more than once. I fell asleep next to her a few days ago, after fucking her for hours, and neither of us woke up until the next morning. So what, I thought. An accident. It won't happen again.

But it did. And then it became a deliberate choice, making it all the worse.

She's still asleep now, her face covered by her dark ash blonde mane, her lips partly opened as she lies curled up next to me.

I place a kiss on her cheek, tugging on the collar to see if she's awake. She groans a sweet little complaint, her naked body squirming around in the sheets.

"Time to get up, my pet," I whisper. "You'll get a spanking if you're not up within five minutes."

"Ten," she sighs. "Ten, please, Master. I'm so tired."

Her voice is low, her mind barely awake yet.

"Five," I insist, giving her another kiss before I crawl out of the bed I never should have slept in.

She's not your fucking girlfriend, and she never will be.

It seems I can repeat this mantra as often as I wish, but it won't change the way I act around her. Even the marks on her skin can't belie the fact that I've fallen for her way more than a john should fall for his whore.

Eighteen more days. That's how much longer I can pretend that none of my self-imposed rules exist, and do whatever I want with her. That's how long she'll still be mine. After that, it has to stop, all of it.

"Five minutes," I repeat. "Or you won't be able to sit for a week."

She growls, but catches herself just in time.

"Yes, Master," I hear her weak voice from beneath the sheets.

I pull myself away from her and leave the room to head downstairs. Nothing has changed in regard to where she's allowed to be in the house. She's never to leave her room, unless I bring her downstairs to have a meal together, but I always bring her back up to her room right after. She has never seen my bedroom, my office, or any other room in the house. At least that's a distance I manage to maintain.

I'm just about to start the coffee machine when my phone rings. This happens so rarely that the sound startles me, and I almost let the carafe fall to the floor. Who on Earth would call me on a Saturday morning?

The first people that come to mind are my grand-parents. Did something happen to one of them? It's not Sunday. It's not their day to call.

My heart is racing when I head over to the phone, and I'm flooded with relief when I see that it's not their number on the screen.

But the relief is soon replaced with bewildered anger.

It's the agency.

CHAPTER 40

LIANA

T hree weeks. It's been three weeks since he grabbed me off the street, removing me from a life I had come to loathe.

By now, people must be looking for me. I haven't had access to the internet or a TV during the last twenty-one days. But I bet I would see my picture on the local news.

I wonder if Luke had been questioned as a suspect? Kidnapped or killed by the ex-boyfriend, that would be such a classic, and I wouldn't be surprised if he was one of the first to be questioned after it became apparent that I was missing.

How long did it take for anyone to notice? The Monday after my disappearance? Wednesday? Maybe even an entire week? No, I don't believe it would take them that long. I've always been very reliable, an exemplary employee who never skipped work or even took sick leave. I've always shown up at work when I was expected to, always. And if not, I would have called in before anyone even knew that I wasn't there.

But who knows how things are now that Professor Miller is gone? It may have taken them a few days to start worrying about me because everyone is too preoccupied with his death. Or they might have thought that *I'm* overwhelmed by grief and thus unable to show up for work or to call in sick?

My mind has been too preoccupied with what has been happening between me and Joseph to drift away to all the things I left behind. But once in a while, when I'm by myself and not too exhausted or too dazed by a play session, I find myself faced with the reality of what I left behind. The insecurity of unemployment, the grief of losing the nicest boss I could ever ask for, and the pain of a broken relationship. None of that matters here, in this house, in this bedroom.

All that matters is us. Joseph and me.

We have talked a lot during the past week, but I can't talk about these things with him. I can't talk about a job he doesn't know I had because he thinks that I'm a full-time prostitute. I tried to talk about Luke, but it felt wrong, and he cut me short anyway. It must have been the most awkward conversation we've ever had. He seemed to be in agony when I talked about Luke, about the things he said about my sexual desires, about what he did to me to finally make me realize that I needed to kick him out of my life.

I let out a deep sigh and turn off the water in the shower. He will be back soon to bring me downstairs for breakfast, and I need to be dressed and ready.

Each day with him is similar, and yet so different that I can never know what to expect. All I know is that it will entail a lot of pleasure, sometimes pain, sometimes a training session so hard that it makes me question my decision to stay here of my own free will. I can see the effects of his training in the way my body reacts to him. Just the sound of his voice, a look on his face or the most trivial touch can cause my core to throb with desire. I'm often wet before he even touches me. I've grown dependent on him, and that unsettles me.

And I'm getting addicted to all of it. To him especially. I feel like I will never have enough.

That's what scares me the most.

Because I know that all of this will come to an end. He will let me go eventually. I don't know when it will happen, but I know it will.

He thinks I'm a prostitute who's just doing this because he's paying her to. No matter how close I may feel to him, how intimate our time together has become. None of this is real for him, and he's probably done it before, probably many times. He keeps saying that I enjoy special privileges, but he may say such things to all the girls.

I shake my head, chasing away uncomfortable truths. All those things are future Liana problems. She'll be able to deal with it.

All I have to focus on is today, and I don't have much time left to get ready before he shows up for breakfast.

I've just stepped out of the shower and in the process of drying myself off, when I can hear footsteps outside in the hall.

Oh my God, he's back already!

I hurry to wrap the towel around myself and scurry out of the bathroom, falling to my knees in the bedroom just as he opens the door.

Something is off, I can tell right away. The way he swings the door open, the way he's breathing so erratically.

I lift my eyes up to him, confused at his exasperated behavior.

My breath catches when I see his face. His cheeks are blazing red, his hair messed up as if he's ruffled through his black strands a few times frantically, and he's panting like he's in a panic. I barely recognize him. He has never looked like this. Horrified, confused, and angry, all at once. Something must be terribly wrong.

Our eyes lock on each other as he freezes a few feet away from me. I'm sitting on the floor, positioned the way I was trained to sit, with my palms on my thighs and sitting back on my heels.

I want to ask him what it is. I want to know what's wrong.

But I can't find my voice. His troubled hazel eyes speak of too much terror.

I don't dare ask because I'm scared of the answer.

CHAPTER 41

JOSEPH

Why the fuck would they call me? That has never happened before—because it's not *supposed* to happen. Everything is clearly stated in the contract. There's to be absolutely no contact between the agency and me, or the agency and her.

Unless there's an emergency.

But how could there be an emergency? Everything is going perfect, almost too perfect, with Ruby.

For a moment, I consider not picking up because this must clearly be a mistake. But not picking up would be another breach. I've agreed to answering if they try to reach me, no matter what. I have to pick up.

"Yes," I say, sounding as irritated as I am.

"Mr. Bennett?" a female voice at the other end asks.

It's Lisa, the woman who handles the 'contacts,' as they call them. She has been my contact person for every part of this transaction.

"Yes, of course it's me," I bark at her.

"This is Lisa speaking, from Violent Delights—"

"I know," I interrupt her. "What's wrong? Why are you calling me?"

Lisa clears her throat, letting precious seconds pass before she replies.

"Mr. Bennett, I'm surprised we didn't hear back from you already," she says. "We were just contacted by Miss Ruby Red, and she said she was never picked up. I don't know why she waited this long to inform us, but I'm even more surprised you never let us know that the arrangement was off?"

Her words knocked every wisp of air from my lungs. I stand motionless, not even breathing, as my blood runs cold through my veins and the words bounce back and forth in my skull.

They were contacted by a woman named Ruby Red.

The woman I bought to play my slave. The woman who's supposed to be upstairs right now, waiting for my return.

And she said she's never been picked up.

"Mr. Bennett?"

"Are you... are you sure?" I stutter, my voice cracking on every word.

Lisa appears to be startled by my question.

"Yes, she came to the agency herself and said her time window passed without being picked up," she says. "She's asking for compensation because of the stress and the inconvenience."

I can't reply. I feel as if a clamp is closing around my chest, stealing my breath and robbing me of my ability to speak. My face is stuck in an incredulous expression with an unblinking stare as my brain desperately scrambles to make sense of this.

"Did something come up?" Lisa asks, breaking into my stunned stupor. "How come you never contacted us? Is something wrong?"

She clears her throat, pausing for a moment before she continues speaking.

"Mr. Bennett, if there's anything wrong with Miss Red, you'll have to tell us. Is she telling the truth? Did something about her not please you? If so, why didn't you let us know?"

I'm still rendered speechless, my mouth opening and shutting like a goldfish with no sound coming out, as I try to gather myself. I fail to comprehend what's happening, managing only a stunned shake of my head as the woman on the other end of the line starts losing her patience.

"Mr. Bennett?" she presses. "Are you still with me?"

I have to say something. Something.

My first instinct is to tell her that this must be a mistake because there is a Ruby Red in my house right now, and she has been here for the past three weeks, just as agreed upon.

Everything is fine.

Everything is fucking fine.

Except that it's not.

"Mr. Bennett, I—"

"Yes, it's fine," I croak. "It's… something came up. Family emergency. I'm sorry, I was too preoccupied to contact the agency."

"Oh, I see," Lisa says. She's not sounding convinced, but if there's one thing these guys are good at, it's discretion.

"Pay the girl the compensation," I tell her.

"Okay, thank you, Mr. Bennett," she says. "I'll get things sorted with her. Please, could you let us know next time? I know how stressful things like this can be, but we're working in a very delicate business here. With very delicate subjects."

I roll my eyes, unbeknownst to her.

"Yes, I'm sorry for the trouble," I tell her. "But I have one question. This Ruby girl, did she do what she was told to, during the days when her window was open?"

"According to her, she did," Lisa tells me. "She's been out and about, wearing everything that she was asked to."

I had just been able to breathe again, when her words take the air out of my lungs anew.

Ruby, or whoever she is, didn't wear any of the things I asked. She didn't wear stockings under her skirt, and she didn't understand why I got so mad at her in the beginning. She didn't follow the most mundane commands, and she looked at me with a terror that looked so real it was bone-chilling.

It looked real, because it *was* real.

I made a mistake. *I kidnapped the wrong woman.*

How could this fucking happen?

"Oh, but she did mention something," Lisa interrupts my distressed stream of thoughts. "Her red coat was stolen one night. I believe it was meant to be her token?"

Yes.

That fucking coat.

I'd watched her run around in that coat for days, I watched her enter a bar wearing that same coat, and I watched her come out of that same bar in that very same coat.

Or so I thought.

"It was stolen in a bar?" I ask.

"Yes, I think that's what she said," Lisa says, sounding surprised. "How did you-?"

"Just a guess," I hurry to say. "Listen. I have business to attend. Will you handle Miss Ruby and let her know I'm very sorry for the trouble?"

"Yes, sure," she replies. "So, I shouldn't file for a new arrangement?"

"No, not at this moment," I tell her. "Goodbye."

I don't wait for her final words before I end the call and throw the damn phone across the room. The noise as it hits the floor echoes through the hall, piercing through my head like a thousand knives.

My chest is still tight, a cold wrath of panic closing in on me as I try to gather together the pieces of this fucked-up mix-up.

She's not Ruby Red. She even fucking *told* me, she's not her.

"Do you think I'm Ruby?" she said. *"Because I'm not."*

But I was too occupied to listen, too certain, too immersed in the game. Just like her when she first got here, I'm overwhelmed with questions—the most salient one banging against my skull with urgent precedence.

If the girl upstairs is not Ruby Red, then who the hell is she?

CHAPTER 42

LIANA

"You stole that coat," he says, pointing a trembling finger at me.

My heart stops in shock.

He knows.

I don't know what happened after he left my room. I don't know what or who tipped him off. But I know that he knows.

He knows I'm not the woman he thought I was.

I stare up at him, my mouth partly opening as I try to come up with a reply, but the words escape me.

"You stole that red fur coat," he repeats, putting emphasis on every word. *"Didn't you?"*

"You're scaring me, Master—"

"Tell me!" he interrupts me.

I hurry to nod. "Yes, I did."

His face changes again, now displaying the despair of someone who just lost something valuable forever.

"You're not Ruby Red," he whispers.

It's not a question, but a statement. Yet I reply by shaking my head.

"I'm not," I whisper.

He's struggling for breath, and throwing his arms up in the air.

"I fucked up," he gasps, short of breath. "I *so* fucking fucked up."

I don't know what to say, so I just remain in my spot, my fists clenching around the towel that I have wrapped around my body.

"My name is Liana," I say in a low voice. "I told you."

"Fuck," he says. "Fuck! Fuck! *Fuuuck*!"

I flinch when he raises his arms again, but he only does it to ruffle through his wild hair, holding his head with his hands as he stalks, pacing back and forth through the room.

"Fuck!" he continues cursing. "This is not fucking happening!"

He's so loud and so wildly distraught that I'm scared of him for the first time in weeks. I want to move out of his range, but I don't even dare get up on my feet.

Suddenly, he stops mid-motion, freezing for a moment, before he turns back to me, looking at me with worry painted across his face that is unlike anything I've seen on him before.

"I'm so fucking sorry," he says. "I made a mistake. I fucked up so badly."

He approaches me, going down on his knees in front of me, so we're almost on eye level as his gaze fixates on mine.

"I thought you were someone else," he explains. "A woman named Ruby Red. I… hired her to do all of this. To role play with me."

I bite my lower lip. Well, there you go. I was right.

"She… you were wearing that coat," he adds, gesturing over to the hideous fur coat that's hanging over the end of the bed. "That was the token that helped me recognize her. That coat. *You* had that coat, and the business card, and—"

"I know," I interrupt him. "I know."

He halts, staring at me with eyes widened in surprise.

"What do you mean?" he asks.

"I… I know what happened," I utter. "I mean, I didn't know at first, but I've known now for a while. I figured it out."

His facial expression changes from bewilderment to fury.

"You *what*?!" he yells at me.

I wince at his outburst, pulling the towel further up my chest as if I was trying to protect myself from his rage.

"It's okay," I say, raising my hand in a soothing gesture to match my words. "I'm not mad at you. We're good."

He raises his eyebrows, looking at me as if I just suggested we jump off a cliff together.

"We're *good*?!" he exclaims. "You fucking lied to me! How did you even know? Did you trick me?"

"Trick you?" I ask. "No! It's nothing like that. It was a simple mistake. You thought I was that Barbie doll at the bar, the woman whose coat I was wearing."

He looks at me through narrowed eyes, and I can tell that it takes all his strength to contain his anger. He's clenching his fists and breathing erratically.

"I had no idea what was going on," I add. "I couldn't make sense of anything, before I realized—"

"When?" he interrupts me. "When did you realize what's been going on here?"

Our eyes lock on each other in a tense stare. He's about an arm's length away from me. I hate the distance between us. I want to curl up in his embrace and go back to the place where we were just a few minutes ago. A place that was overshadowed by a lie, but a safe and warm place, nonetheless.

"When you called me Ruby," I say. "That's when I had a suspicion that you might think I was someone else."

My words cause a frown to form on his face.

"I mean, I didn't *know* for sure," I try to save myself. "But there were so many things that suggested a mix-up. You always acted as if I should know what was going on, as if I should know how to—"

"But you *didn't* know, did you?" he hisses. "You thought I was just a fucked-up criminal who'd rape and kill you."

I look at him, knowing that his words are true, but it seems like so much time has passed since I was stricken with that terror. He was a different person to me back then.

I was a different person.

"In the beginning, yes, but—"

"You *made* me a criminal!" he interrupts me. "And I am. What I did to you was wrong, and you *knew* it was wrong. You lied to me and made me believe that things were happening exactly as they were supposed to happen."

He pauses, clearing his throat before he continues speaking in that same threatening tone.

"What's your end game here?" he wants to know. "Did you want to blackmail me? Threaten to sue me so you could squeeze out some money from the twisted wealthy idiot?"

"What? No!" I object. "How could you say that?"

His accusations hurt. Does he really think I was playing him? Does none of this mean anything to him?

"How could I *say* that?" he barks, scaring me as he straightens up, continuing to pace up and down the length of the room.

I watch him as he tries to process his boiling rage. He's panting and growling in anger, looking almost as if he was in pain.

He probably is.

CHAPTER 43

LIANA

"Joseph, please—"

"Don't call me that!" he yells, pointing at me from afar. "It was a mistake to ever tell you my name. I never should have done that. All of this. All of this was a huge fucking mistake!"

His voice is so loud and filled with pain that I can feel it rumbling in my own heavy chest.

"Please—"

I'm interrupted by him punching the wall next to the dresser. The sheer brutality of his fist ramming into the wall makes me jump to my feet and hurry away from him, clutching the towel around my body.

He's hyperventilating, his fist flying into the wall again and again, with so much force that plaster is falling down around him. But the biggest damage is what he's inflicting on himself. His knuckles are leaving bloody prints on the white wall as he keeps punching it in a furious rampage. He's growling with every punch, but it's not the pain of the impact that tortures him.

His agony runs deeper than that.

"Stop it!" I yell at him from afar. "Jose—"

I stop and correct myself. "Master! Stop it! You're hurting yourself!"

He keeps going, his bloody fist slamming into the wall again and again. Each impact feels like a dagger to my heart. Seeing him hurt himself over something I did to him is too much to bear. I'm choking, my heart racing in panic, as I watch helplessly.

I can't let this happen. I need to stop him.

"Master!" I yell again, this time running toward him. His destructive frenzy scares the hell out of me, but my worry for him overpowers any sense of fear I might have for my own safety.

"Master," I say again, trying to calm my voice to a soothing tone, as I let go of the towel and wrap my arms around him from behind, evading his vicious fist. My embrace is fueled with trust and empathy running stronger than fright. My only concern is for him, his safety, his sanity.

His body is hard and tense when I first force my touch on him, but I can feel him relax instantly. The towel falls to the floor, leaving me naked and exposed as I press myself against his strong and rough body.

His fist comes to a halt, pressed against the wall while his breathing settles to a calmer rhythm.

"Master," I whisper. "Please, don't do this to yourself. You're hurting me more than you hurt yourself."

He's shaking, slowly moving his fist away from the wall, while his other hand finds mine, grasping it in a tight grip. I flinch in surprise when he turns around in a sudden motion, pulling me toward him in a close embrace. I know he doesn't want me to see it, but I notice the threat of tears shimmering in his eyes before he pulls me in for a kiss, taking my face between both his hands while our tongues entwine in desperate need for each other.

I can smell the blood on his knuckles as it gets smeared across my cheek, mixing with the tears that are running down my face.

He breaks our kiss, staring into my teary eyes with a gaze of dark significance.

"You have to leave," he whispers.

I gasp in shock.

"No," I object. "I don't want to leave."

But he shakes his head.

"You *have* to leave, now," he insists. "I'll pay you whatever you ask for, but you cannot stay here. Not after what has happened."

"What?" I breathe. "You can't be serious."

I place my hands on his, wincing as I touch the blood on his right knuckles.

"Master, I don't want to leave," I say, my lips trembling as I suppress the urge to cry. "I want to stay here. I lo—"

"No," he interrupts, shaking me. "You betrayed me. You made me a criminal. You *knew,* and you didn't tell me. This was supposed to be *my* game, *my* rules, under *my* control. You took all of that away from me and made the game yours."

I try to shake my head at his accusations, but I can't because he still holds me in a tight grip.

He pauses, adding a hysteric laugh between his ranting.

"I gave you a fucking *collar,*" he adds. "A fucking collar."

I choke up under another rush of tears that takes away my ability to speak.

"You may not be a whore, but you can't be trusted," he hisses. "You bewitched me like a fucking succubus. You made me lose myself, and play fucking boyfriend and girlfriend with you. I fell for your fucking tricks. You made me believe things that weren't there."

"That's not true!" I disagree. "I never tricked you. I didn't mean for this to happen, but I never *played* you. Everything has been honest and real. Everything we did was true—"

"No!" he barks. "It was all based on a lie, an imbalance of knowledge that put you in power. You fucking witch!"

I'm sobbing in his hold, simultaneously glaring up at him with determination. He's angry, but I can tell that he's not really angry at me. He's angry at himself.

"The only person who fell for anything was me," I say through compressed lips. "I fell for *you*. I may not be the woman you ordered, but I *want* to be yours."

I halt for a moment, trying to regain my composure.

"I'm *proud* to wear your collar," I say in a suppressed whisper. "I don't do it because you pay me to."

Despite the ferocity of a hurt beast still apparent in his gaze, I can see him softening to my words. He has every reason to feel betrayed, and he's told me enough about himself and his past to enable me to make sense of this outburst.

He's all about control, a safe setting, an agreed upon arrangement, set in a safe and consensual setting. His mistake and my knowledge about it turned all of this upside down.

He needs to know that he's not to blame, and that I had to intention of playing him.

"You might have made a mistake," I breathe, fixating on his tormented gaze. "You didn't take the woman you ordered, but you did take the *right* woman."

His eyes flicker with confusion.

"This was meant to happen," I add. "It's what I've always wanted."

JOSEPH

She's still doing it. Her spell is still working on me.

Her words, her touch, all of it embraces me with a soothing warmth that terrifies me to the bone. This shouldn't be happening. None of this.

I haven't lost control like this in years, and it's all because of her.

"You betrayed me," I accuse her again. It takes all my strength not to let her tears get to me. Who knows if they're real? Who knows if anything she says or makes me feel is real? She's a liar.

She touches my hands, seemingly unfazed by the blood that's running down one of them.

"I didn't want to betray you," she says. "I wanted to be with you. That's why I didn't say anything. I was scared you'd make me leave."

She pauses, biting her lower lip, as she seeks my eyes with a pained face.

"And now you are," she utters. "Now you want me to leave."

I let go of her. She's robbing me of my sanity. I need room to breathe, room to process the extent of what has happened with her.

I kidnapped a woman. I took her away from her life. There might even be a police report on her.

"People are searching for you," I tell her. "You need to go home. You need to get away from me."

"No!" she protests, wrapping her arms around her naked body. "I want to stay—"

"You can't!" I yell at her. "We can't act as if this was okay, as if it was right for me to bring you here, to make you my slave, to fuck you, to…"

I stop myself before I say something truly stupid. But she finishes the sentence for me.

"To love me," she whispers, her eyes glistening with tears as she casts me a hurt look. "Isn't that what you were going to say?"

I look at her, swallowing the emotions her appearance evokes within me. She has blood running down one side of her face, my blood, mixing with her salty tears. Her hair is still damp from the shower, sticking to her slim shoulders in stray strands, her smooth body exposed to me as she steps closer to me.

She's insane. She must be, if she still wants to be with me after what I've done to her. There's no other explanation. And her next words only prove me right.

"Lock me up," she says. "In the attic. Punish me."

"What?" I bark at her. "Are you fucking ins—"

"I don't care how long it takes for you to forgive me," she stops me. "But I know I deserve to be punished."

She pauses, taking another step forward, pressing her naked body against me.

"Let me prove to you that I want to be yours," she breathes. "Punish me. Lock me up in the attic until I'm forgiven."

"You have lost your mind if you think that I'd actually do that," I hiss at her. "You have lost your fucking mind."

I put distance between us, walking backwards as if she was posing a threat to me. Her eyes follow me, dazed with sorrow and fear, and terrifyingly clear at the same time.

I can't deal with this. I shouldn't. She's already taken too much from me. She needs to get out of here.

"Get cleaned up and dressed," I tell her. "I will drive you home."

Her face migrates to an expression of utter shock. She darts toward me, but this time I won't let her catch me. I raise my hand, pointing my finger at her as a warning.

"Pet!" I yell at her, causing her to stop mid-motion. "Get cleaned up and dressed *now*."

I can see her struggling to obey. She's been trained well enough to feel an instant urge to comply with what

I say when I address her that way. It's become part of her nature, a natural instinct that tells her to follow her Master's wish and receive pleasure in return.

There's no pleasure attached to my current command, but the need to serve is still there.

"You'll get dressed now," I repeat my words, still pointing my finger at her. "Do you understand?"

She glares at me through narrowed and saddened eyes, processing my words with furious determination. I don't even know what to wish for. To hear the words from her lips? *Yes, Master.* It would mean that she's following my order, but it would also mean that she agrees to leave.

I look at her, standing there, completely naked, hugging herself because no one else does, blood and tears running down her precious cheeks, in desperate need of her Master's touch. And I'm denying it to her.

It breaks me to see her like this. I need to leave the room before things go horribly awry. I can hear her sobbing behind me when I pull my eyes away and head for the door to leave.

As soon as I turn the knob and open the door, I can hear her steps on the carpet, closing in on me with hectic speed. Just as I turn around, wanting to beckon her to stop, she darts right past me, slipping through by ducking underneath my stretched out arm and running down the corridor.

My eyes follow her, my body turning still as I watch her run toward the attic door.

CHAPTER 45

LIANA

I don't even know what I'm trying to do. It's like a switch has been turned on inside my head, leaving all control to my legs as they carry me to the room I've been so desperate to get out of. For all I know, it won't even be accessible. Every door around me has been locked for the past three weeks.

But this one is not. I'm relieved and surprised when the door actually swings open when I throw myself against it with a little too much force. I stumble into the room, taking a moment to regain my balance, before I manage to close the door behind me.

It can't be locked or unlocked from the inside, I remember that much from my very first night here. I let the door shut and immediately fling myself against the shabby wood, using my own body weight to keep him from entering.

My heart is racing as wild thoughts bounce back and forth inside my skull.

What the hell am I doing? I'm completely naked, my hair is still wet from the shower, blood and tears are drying on my cheeks, and all I wish for is to be locked away in this hellhole?

The room is just as empty and cold as it was three weeks ago. It's unwelcoming to begin with, but an even more terrible place to be in, in my state.

My skin is covered in goosebumps within seconds, and my bare feet hurt against the rough wooden floor. Outside, I can hear his hurried steps approaching.

I yelp when he bangs against the door from the outside, shaking my entire body with his savagery.

"Get out!" he screams from the other side of the door.

"No!" I yell back at him. "You're breaking the rules. I deserve to be punished."

I was hoping that he'd jump on board if I retreated to the contract he apparently laid out with the woman who was supposed to be here in my place.

But it appears he's no longer interested in playing that game.

"You get out of there right now," he repeats. "Or I'll drag you out myself. You know I can."

He bangs against the door again, causing it to open for just a moment before I manage to push it back. My feet slip across the cold wood, and a splinter gets jammed into one of my soles causing agonizing pain.

Another bang against the door almost causes me to fall, and this time it's my back that slides along the harsh wood of the door.

"You're going to hurt me if you break in the door," I warn him. "I thought you promised never to hurt me!"

"Step away!" he yells, sounding beside himself. "You're acting crazy."

Maybe I am. But it's the only thing I know to do. I'll spend the entire day and night like this, if it means he doesn't send me away.

He lets go of the door, and I can hear him taking a step back.

"What do you want from me?" he asks, sounding defeated. "How much do I have to pay for you to let this go and be reasonable?"

I growl in anger.

"I'm not a prostitute!" I remind him. "You won't pay me anything, no matter to what end. I don't want your money."

"What then?" he asks.

I hesitate, biting my lower lip as I stare down at my feet. My toes are beginning to hurt because of the damp cold in this room. I take a deep breath, collecting my strength to go through with this.

I can do this. I can.

My gaze wanders around the small room, the room I wanted to so desperately escape when he first locked me up in here. All of that seems so far away. I can't believe it's only been three weeks since then. It feels like another life, another person who did this to me, another person who all of this happened to. Both of us have changed, and it's thanks to being with each other, to finding one another.

"You know I've fantasized about something like this for the longest time," I say, raising my volume just loud enough for him to hear me on the other side of the door. "In the darkest corner of my mind, I've fantasized about being kidnapped, locked away, tied up and forced to please a handsome man like you."

I close my eyes. Even when there's no one looking at me, it still fills me with shame to admit all these things, to give voice to my darkest fantasies. The same fantasies that caused Luke to be disgusted with me. The memory pains me, but I may need to face it aloud so he'll listen to me.

"You know, my ex-boyfriend, he always said that I was broken because of the way my father treated me and my mother," I say. "He insinuated that I like to be punished because I was hit as a child. But I don't want to believe that, and I don't think it's true."

I pause, listening for him outside the door, to see if he'll interrupt and silence me again. But all I hear is the steady sound of his breath as he waits for me to continue.

"My father was an asshole," I go one. "I'd never want a man to treat me the way he treated my mother and me.

No. I want *this*. I want *you*. I want what you're able to give me."

I hesitate again, trying to hold back the tears as they threaten to choke me up again.

"If you send me away now, I feel like I will lose you forever," I proceed. "And I'd rather rot in here for days than to never see you again."

I can't help but to start sobbing again, another rush of tears running down my face.

Outside, I can hear him moving, but he's not banging against the door this time. He's not hammering against the wood or yelling for me to come out and leave.

"Let me in," he says instead, his voice soft and defeated.

CHAPTER 46

JOSEPH

She lets a few moments pass before she moves away from the door. I turn the knob and push it open carefully, in case she's still standing close to it.

I find her standing in the middle of the room, naked and distraught, with new tears mixing with the dried-up bloody mess on her cheeks.

A violent cry escapes from her chest when I hurry toward her, wrapping my arms around her small body, as I pull her in for a heartfelt embrace.

"I'm sorry," I whisper in her ear, while she cries in my arms.

"You said you'd never hurt me," she whimpers. "You promised."

I close my eyes, my chest heavy with pain as I'm confronted with her agony.

"You have no idea how sorry I am," I repeat. "For everything."

She buries her face in my chest, shaken by brutal sobs as I lift her up and carry her out of the room. Her crying intensifies when she realizes that I'm removing her from the attic, the place she thinks she deserves to be right now.

"You've been punished enough," I tell her as I carry her down the hallway. "My pet."

Her gaze wanders up to me, searching for clarification.

"You're not sending me away?" she asks, hope shining through every syllable of her question.

I shake my head.

"You're insane, crazy, twisted," I tell her. "But you're *my* crazy pet."

I set her down to open the door to her bathroom. "Let's clean you up."

She sniffs and nods, looking so insanely vulnerable and exhausted that I'm overwhelmed with the urge to protect her. No one, especially me, should ever be allowed to make her feel like this. It angers me to know how she's been treated by other men before, her father, her ex-boyfriend. They don't even deserve to breathe the same air as her.

I draw her a bath, and as I reach over to start the water, she gasps in shock next to me.

"Your hand!" she exclaims. "It looks terrible. You need to see a doctor!"

I hadn't even noticed the blood on my knuckles, it only caught my eye when I left traces of it on her beautiful face.

She takes my hand, carefully pulling it closer to her so she can inspect the damage I've done to myself.

"It's nothing," I say, trying to downplay the extent of the injury. "It doesn't even hurt."

She furrows her eyebrows as she looks up at me.

"Where's your medical kit?" she wants to know.

I sigh. "I will take care of it. Don't worry about it."

"Please," she begs. "It's my fault this happened. If you deny me taking care of you, it'd feel like another punishment."

She pauses, her face turning to a focused expression as she contemplates her next move.

"You'd hurt me," she adds. "Not allowing me to take care of you would seriously hurt me."

She can't hide a little smirk on her face when she's speaking those words to me.

"Little minx," I say. "You know you can't play that card every time you want something from me."

Her face changes to a disarming smile as she bats her eyes at me. "But could I today?"

I'm defenseless against her charm and let her do as she wishes. She bandages my hand while we're soaking in the bathtub together. Now that the adrenaline rush is over, I can feel the mundane but stinging pain on my knuckles as she doctors the wounds.

I watch her as the water plays around the curves of her breasts. Just the picture of her, naked and focused as she tends to me, is enough for my cock to crave her. She smiles when she notices my hardness jutting against her thigh.

"Even after all of this?" she asks, winking at me.

"I can't help it," I say. "With such a beautiful pet right in front of me."

She fixates her attention on the bandage around my hand.

"All done," she says, moving my hand to the side of the tub. "Keep it out of the water."

I smile at her, struggling to believe that she's still here. Only a few hours have passed since I learned that she was not the woman I had planned to kidnap.

I *really* kidnapped her, I took her from her life, when she had absolutely no idea that this would happen to her.

That's why everything with her has felt so real from the get-go. Because it *was* real.

She was a real victim to my twisted needs. And yet, she's still here. She still wants to be here, just as I want her to be here.

But that doesn't change the facts we've tried to ignore until now.

"People must be looking for you," I say. "Your friends, your family. If we turn on the news, we might even see you there."

She curves her lips into a sad smile.

"I don't have many friends here," she says. "Most of them were *his* friends, we always hung out together, and I never bothered to make my own friends since I moved here. But yeah, I guess work will miss me, and they probably informed my mother."

"You will have to let them know that you're okay," I tell her.

She nods in agreement. "I know I have to."

"And you need to tell them something about where you were," I add, feeling a heavy lump in my throat as I'm overcome with guilt.

"I'll come up with something," she says, as her hands absentmindedly wander below the surface of the water until she finds my cock.

I sigh when she wraps her hand around it, slowly massaging my length by applying and releasing pressure in turns.

"My life had been pretty bleak in the days leading up to you," she says in a low voice, without stopping what she's doing. "I can always blame it on that. Say things got too much for me and I needed a break from everything, a little retreat, a hiatus from life."

Her eyes find mine, locking onto my gaze as her lips part in an alluring motion.

"Is that why you were at that bar that night?" I ask her. "To drown your sorrows?"

She nods. "Yes, I guess you could say that."

"And what made you steal that coat?" I want to know.

Her eyelashes flutter, while her mouth tips into a coy smile.

"Maybe I knew it would lead me to you."

CHAPTER 47

LIANA

Day thirty-nine. Today is the day when everything was supposed to end.

He told me everything, and filled me in on every little detail about this arrangement I had involuntarily become a part of. He told me about the agency, about the agreement that there would be no communication between him and them once the girl was in his house, about the girl's requirements, and the settings and rules they agreed to before consenting to become his slave.

He also told me how much they'd be paid once the thirty-nine days were over. It was enough for them to never have to work again, which most likely served as the biggest incentive for most of them.

"And you never fell in love with any of them?" I asked him at one point.

Joseph shook his head.

"I was done with them as soon as the contract was over," he said. "They usually bored me at that point anyway."

I also asked him if any of them ever fell in love with him. The thought that he has done this with quite a few women before me left a sting in my heart, and I'd be surprised if all of them had been as untouched by the entire thing as he claims they were.

"I don't know," he said. "Maybe. It never concerned me."

His words were cold, but earnest. It's still hard for me to believe that I, of all women, should be the one to crack his hard shell, but once I did, I found a core so gentle, wise and loving that I never stood a chance.

The last eighteen days were like an early honeymoon, a retreat for two broken souls who selfishly took the time to grow with each other.

I never left his house until this day. I begged him to allow us to complete the deal as arranged, since there was no urgent reason for me to show up anywhere.

I no longer have a job to return to, and another secretary was hired to deal with the aftermath of Professor Miller's death. There was nothing left for me to do, as most other issues could only be dealt with by the academic staff.

Calling my mother was the hardest part. She had a major freak-out when she heard my voice on the phone, and after her initial shock was over, she soon migrated to fury over my "infantile behavior". It was the first time that I told her about the break-up with Luke and losing my job. That's how disconnected we are.

"Do you have any idea what it's like to be called by the police in the middle oft he night? Telling you that your daughter has been missing for days, and then giving you those reproachful hints when you have no idea where she might be?" she asked, her annoyance palpable. She didn't know about any of the trouble that had befallen my life, but once I told her, she sighed with understanding.

"I'm just glad you're alive," she concluded after I gave her that half-assed explanation, in a tone that insinuated that she was mostly glad to no longer have to worry about me because it disrupted her own life.

It's all well and done.

I woke up next to Joseph every single day, our nervous hearts intertwining more and more with every moment we spent together. This was the most intense way to start a relationship, but it works for us.

But today, things will change. Today is when our contract ends.

Today is also the day I will lose my collar and have it replaced with something else. When he told me that he would have to take the collar away from me, I choked up a little because it felt as if he was telling me he would rip a part of my heart out once we reached day thirty-nine.

I have to say goodbye to a lot of things today to make room for the new. We've already packed up the red fur coat and mailed it back to its owner. I wonder if she ever figured out that I was the one who took it, if she even noticed me at all. It felt wrong to keep the coat, even though I know she has been paid a generous amount as compensation despite never having to go through with her end of the deal. As ugly as it may be, the red fur coat has become special to me, not only because it was the reason for me to end up here, but also because it kept me warm and protected when I needed it most.

Just like that cold and dark time, the coat is now a part of my past and I no longer need it.

I'm down in the kitchen standing in front of the French doors, daydreaming as my eyes wander along the landscape outside. I'm no longer confined to the space upstairs. He's shared his home with me as if it was the most natural thing to do. And in a way, with us, it is.

He told me that he usually has some staff around the house, but I've only met one of them, his house maid Marjory. She's a sweet, middle-aged lady who's driving a red sedan, the car I saw driving up to the house the day he left me alone. She had been working for his grandparents before they left for Florida and has been an integral part of Joseph's life for a very long time, which is why meeting her made me just as nervous as if I was about to meet his mother. She seemed surprised to see me, and it was more than awkward to know that she was in the know about who I was and how I ended up to be in the house. However, she never said anything about it and treated me as if I had entered Joseph's life like any other girlfriend would.

"Are you ready?" I hear his voice behind my back.

I turn around and find him looking as magnificent as always, dressed in his navy blue suit, my favorite on him because it brings out his dark hazel eyes and hugs his masculine frame perfectly. He's freshly shaved and has his hair gelled and styled to the nines, making me feel underwhelmingly dressed, despite the new Miu Miu dress I'm wearing. It's a present from him to mark the end of our first thirty-nine days together, a kind of anniversary that no other couple would celebrate.

"Yes," I say, but it's a lie.

I knew I couldn't flee from my responsibilities forever, I knew this day would come. But I never felt less ready for anything in my life. I wish I could hide in this strange getaway forever, hugged by his strong arms, feeling the warmth of his body pressed against mine, and his cock throbbing inside me. There's no place I'd rather be.

He comes to a halt next to me, brushing a strand of hair back over my shoulder, while his eyes focus on my neck. I swallow hard, preparing myself for something I don't want to happen.

"Today marks an end," he says, as his hands wander to the little heart-shaped lock at the front. "And the beginning of something new."

His words are concluded by the clicking sound of the lock as he opens it. I sigh when he slowly removes the collar from around my neck. My hand moves up imme-diately, touching the unfamiliar emptiness around my throat.

"I'll miss it," I whisper, casting him a sad look.

He smiles at me.

"You're still my pet," he promises. "But today, we have some things to take care of. Come."

He puts the collar aside and takes my hand to lead me outside.

CHAPTER 48

JOSEPH

S he's shy about letting me see her apartment when we first get there, and already begins to make excuses about its alleged chaos when we're still in the car. It's cute to see her this flustered about showing me a part of her that's new to me.

Her hand is visibly shaking when she unlocks the door for us, and she casts me an apologetic smile as she beckons me to follow her inside.

"Please, remember no one has been here for more than a month, there might be dust and—"

"Dead plants?" I ask, nodding toward a sad-looking fern on a dresser in her corridor.

She laughs and shakes her head. "Oh no, that's been dead for a while."

Her place is small, but very homey. I don't think I've ever lived in a place like this, small and simple, but so affectionately decorated that it reflects the character of its inhabitant. I don't understand why she would make excuses for any sort of mess because she's clearly a very organized person. Everything matches, everything has its place, even the pen and notebook next to her phone are lined up parallel to the edge of the little table they're lying on.

She keeps casting me insecure looks as she leads me through her place, and I hate that she feels the need to excuse any of it or even feels inferior to me. She has no reason to.

"I love it," I say, as my eyes rest on a few photos she pinned on the wall in her living room. Most of them don't show people, but places and landscapes.

"Oh, that's... I didn't have time to remove those," she hastily says, covering one of the photos that shows her with the guy I assume is her ex-boyfriend.

I smile at her, gently taking her hand and pulling her close to me.

"Relax, my pet," I tell her. "You're mine now, but we both have a past that we shouldn't be afraid to share."

She huffs. "You're one to talk."

"Touché," I say, giving her a kiss on the cheek.

"Do you want something to drink?" she asks. "I could make you a tea or something."

I shake my head.

"I'll be fine, just do what you came here to do," I reply. "I'll wait here and just invade your privacy so I can learn everything about you that there is to learn." I wink.

She furrows her eyebrows, but beckons for me to sit on her small couch.

"Alright, have fun," she says, before she leaves the room.

On her way out, I can see her checking the answering machine on her phone. She flips through the messages without listening to them, looking distraught.

"Are you okay?" I ask.

She sighs, shaking her head.

"Yes, fine," she says without looking at me. "It's just... him."

"He must have been worried, too," I say, assuming she's talking about her ex-boyfriend.

"I guess so," she retorts, before disappearing into her bedroom.

I take a seat, my eyes scanning the room as I try to imagine the life she was leading before I ripped her from it. The kind of woman she was, what her daily routine looked like. It's obvious that she's an avid reader. The bookshelf that covers most of the wall to my right is filled to the brim with books of all genres, but her favorites seem to be thrillers and psychological crime fiction. That shouldn't surprise me.

She's a good and timid girl who's worked hard to keep her life in line, well organized and responsible. But her mind is in a constant struggle, yearning for a breakout from all of this. She's told me about her dark fantasies and how I—unknowingly—made them come true. The terror she felt was real when I kidnapped her, but it excited her as much as it scared her.

For every sick person out there with these dark desires and needs, there is someone else who is willing to serve those demands. I found my match in her.

She has changed clothes when she returns from her bedroom, and is now wearing a black dress, topped with silk tights and a black flower in her ash blonde hair.

"I'm sorry," she says. "I just thought this would be more suitable for…"

She bites her lip and lowers her eyes. I know that this is harder for her than she wants to let on.

"Don't worry about it," I tell her. "I think you're right. And you look lovely no matter what."

"I will change back into the dress you gave me, once we're… done," she promises.

I get up from the couch, placing my hands on her shoulders.

"Look at me, my pet," I command her.

She raises her eyes up to mine, sadness reflected in their gray-blue depths.

"Don't *ever* apologize for yourself," I say. "Especially for something like this."

She nods. "Yes, Master."

Our lips meet for a slow and soft kiss, comforting in ways that words could never be. My hand rests below her ear, while my thumb caresses her cheek as our breaths mingle. I don't break our kiss until I know I can no longer resist the urge to want more. We have things to attend to.

"Are you ready?" I ask her, and she nods, a sad smile fleeting across her face.

The drive to the cemetery is long and filled with pensive silence. Liana is sitting next to me with a white French daisy bouquet resting in her lap, as she stares out the window. She takes a deep breath when we pull up to the cemetery and I park the car.

"Do you want to be by yourself?" I ask her, before she opens the door.

She looks at me, her face already lined with a sorrow I cannot take away from her.

"No," she says after a moment. "Please come with me."

"Alright."

I walk next to her while we follow the directions she's been given to find his grave. She's gripping my hand tightly, while pressing the flowers against her chest with the other.

"I've never had to say goodbye to someone," she says in barely more than a whisper. "Not like this."

"It's the hardest thing we as people have to endure, if you ask me," I say. "It's bad enough to be aware of our own mortality, but to be faced with it when we have to say goodbye to others is even worse."

I can feel her eyes on me from the side, but am not ready to return the look.

"I'm sorry," she says. "I forgot that you've had a much harder parting in your life."

I shake my head.

"It was hard," I say. "But it's true what they say about time. It's the only thing that really can heal all wounds. Even the ones that run as deep as mine."

She squeezes my hand in lieu of a reply. We walk a few more steps in silence, not encountering another person, which is probably because of the murky weather. It's foggy and cold, providing a perfectly gloomy atmosphere in this deserted cemetery.

"This is it," she says, as she stops in front of a newer-looking tombstone.

She freezes in front of it, her lips parted as she lets go of my hand.

"Professor Miller," she whispers, and as soon as she says the name, a tear rolls down her pale cheek.

I want to touch her, hug her, take the pain of grief away from her, but I know I can't. This is something she will have to overcome herself, and I know she will.

There are many things I *can* do for her, though. And I vow to do every single one of them.

I'm relieved to see her smiling as she goes down on her knees to place the bouquet on the grave.

"A tombstone that looks like an opened book," she says, directed toward the grave. "Just plain and simple, with no silly quote. I bet you're glad they didn't bother with any of that nonsense."

She gets back up on her feet, still smiling.

"He hated it when people expressed themselves with quotes," she explains, wiping away her tears as she turns to me. "He always called it lazy."

I smile. "Smart man."

"He was, very straightforward, and a great mentor," she tells me. "I'm going to miss him."

I wrap my arm around her, pulling her closer, while she finally gets a chance to grieve the man who was more than just a boss to her.

We stay for a few more minutes, standing mostly in silence. I want to give her all the time she needs, and wait until she asks to leave.

"Goodbye," she says as we turn away from the grave.

Her words are heavy with meaning, addressing not only her former boss but an entire life she leaves behind.

Then we turn to head back toward the car and the new life that awaits us

LIANA

"Are you sure this is okay?" I ask, nervously playing with my new dress. "And my hair? You don't think I should do more with it?"

Joseph fixes the cuff on his suit and smiles at me through the reflection in the mirror.

"You look fantastic, Liana," he says. "Stop worrying so much."

"Mhm," I say, trying to catch my delirious breath.

I pace up and down the width of the bedroom, trying to think of things I still have to do before we drive to the airport, but there's nothing left. Nothing needs to be cleaned, baked, prepared. There's nothing to occupy my busy mind.

"You are so adorable," Joseph comments from across the room, now walking over to me. "What are you so worried about?"

I look up at him. It's been six months since we've come to the end of our arrangement. Six months during which I turned my life around with his help.

Despite our uninterrupted first thirty-nine days together, I was reluctant to move in with him when he asked me to. I've made the mistake of moving too fast before. Luke and I moved in together after only knowing each other for a few weeks, and I swore to myself that I wouldn't repeat that same mistake.

Of course, with Joseph things are different. So very different. It was a stubborn certainty that things would fall apart that kept me from agreeing to do the thing that felt truly natural with him. This house had become my home before I was even willing to let it happen. It's outside the city, the countryside, a place I never thought I'd want to live.

But things change. I changed. I've come to love the calm landscape, the beautiful estate surrounding our mansion, the gardens and the sound of birds replacing the constant rush of traffic that I'm used to. Besides, the city with all its hustle and bustle is not far away.

Saying goodbye to the apartment that carried so many bad memories of my former relationship was the easiest part of all. I was glad to leave it behind.

Yet I've only officially been living with him for two months now, and I still catch myself calling it his home instead of ours. For some reason, Joseph thought that this would change once we invite two people who'd welcome me into this home just as much as he does.

His grandparents. The people who raised him and who turned his life around for the better.

They're on their way here now, and we are about to leave for Logan Airport to pick them up.

"I'm just so nervous," I say, my entire body shaking. "I mean, meeting family, that's huge. And, it's *you*. Your grandparents."

He chuckles and places a kiss on my cheek.

"You say that as if I was someone to be scared of," he whispers. "Or them."

I shake my head.

"I just want them to like me," I say, knowing how silly that must sound.

"They'll *love* you," he promises. "I mean, I do. I never thought I'd deserve to be loved by a woman like you. And I didn't think I was capable of giving love in return."

He pauses, his dark hazel eyes fixating on mine with intent.

"You proved me wrong," he adds. "If I can't resist your charm, how could anyone else, especially my grandparents?"

He kisses me again, his finger tracing along the sterling silver that adorns my neck.

I'm wearing my day collar, a subtle silver chain with a ring-shaped decor at the front. It sits rather snugly around my throat, but other than that, it can pass off as just another piece of jewelry. An innocent necklace my loving boyfriend bought for me.

I was a little heartbroken when he took my collar away on that day we left his house together for the first time. But he soon replaced it with this, after giving me a few days to decide whether I really wanted to be with him, all things considered.

I didn't need those few days, but I took them anyway, trying to sort out my life and even considering what it would be like without him in it.

But I knew I couldn't return to my old life. I knew it when I said my goodbye at the cemetery, and that certainty only grew during the days I had to spend away from him to think about everything.

I'm perfectly happy where I am right now. *Happy*, not just content.

And that's something I've never been able to say before.

"You're sure they won't notice?" I ask him, pointing to my collar.

He shakes his head.

"You'd have to know what it is to understand," he says. "And if you know what it is, you don't ask about it."

He pauses and laughs.

"Besides, I highly doubt my grandparents are in to any of this," he adds. "They're good people."

"Oh, and we're not?" I ask him teasingly.

Joseph places his palm against my cheek, smiling lovingly at me.

"No, my pet," he says in a soft voice. "We are *us*."

THE END

ABOUT LINNEA

Linnea May loves to read and write about strong alpha men with loaded bank accounts and skeletons in their closets. Her heroes are as sexy and beautiful as they are broken—only to be fixed by the smart & captivating heroines who cross their paths.

Originally from Europe, Linnea currently tries to befriend the lively squirrels in Rhode Island.

ALSO BY LINNEA MAY
(SELECTION)

Violent Cravings: A Dark Billionaire Romance
TAMED: A Bad Boy Billionaire Romance
BARRED: A Bad Boy Billionaire Romance
Master Class
For my Master(s)
His Secret Muse

DARK ROMANCE WITH STELLA NOIR
Silent Daughter: A Dark Billionaire Romance

KEEP IN TOUCH

Sign up to my mailing list to get the latest news about new book releases and to get your FREE short story: **"Anniversary,"** a steamy scene with the protagonists of my other BDSM Romance novel *I Am Yours.*

Linnea's Newsletter:
http://eepurl.com/bb5Z45

Linnea's Author Page:
https://www.amazon.com/Linnea-May/e/
B00RS8VDI0

Made in United States
North Haven, CT
16 July 2023

39151694R00163